Jonathan Rebbeck.

2nd January 1988

READY FOR TAKE-OFF

READY FOR TAKE-OFF

Basic Training for Student Pilots

by

PATRICK QUINN

ROBERT HALE · LONDON

First published in Great Britain 1987

Robert Hale Limited
Clerkenwell House
Clerkenwell Green
London EC1R 0HT

British Library Cataloguing in Publication Data
Quinn, Patrick
Ready for take-off: basic training
for student pilots.
1. Airplanes—Piloting 2. Private flying
I. Title
639.132′5217 TL710

ISBN 0 7090 2998 5

For Vivienne and Lisa,
who decided it's never too late

Filmset in Times by Rowland Phototypesetting Limited
Bury St Edmunds, Suffolk
Printed in Great Britain by
St Edmundsbury Press Limited
Bury St Edmunds, Suffolk
and bound by Hunter & Foulis Limited

Contents

List of Illustrations

Photographs

	Figures	Page
1	The four forces acting on an aircraft in flight	37
2	Air pressure	38
3	Characteristics of a stall	39
4	Control surfaces	40
5	Instrument panel of a Cessna Cutlass. Reproduced by kind permission of the Cessna Aircraft Company	44
6	Effects of the controls	58
7	Rudder and yaw demonstration	59
8	Landing sequence	66

Foreword

A book on aviation is always a welcome addition to my library and one on flying training especially so. Patrick Quinn has written an amusing account of his experiences while learning to fly. His intention is, of course, to transmit the happy fact that learning to fly will be the greatest experience you have ever had 'and this it most certainly will be.' I hope sincerely that those who read his book will be encouraged to take up this great sport which is to many a way of life, but at the same time trust that Patrick's somewhat lighthearted approach will be recognized for what it is and not thought to be always Gospel truth.

I must take issue with him on two points. Personally, I feel that smoking in the aircraft cockpit should be barred completely – it is a fire hazard! At the moment it is legal to smoke and American aircraft manufacturers regrettably encourage the practice by providing ashtrays and cigarette-lighters. My advice is DON'T. The other point concerns R/T. Don't be tempted to throw in the odd pleasantry, keep the chitchat for the ground. If you like the controller, buy him a drink when he is off duty.

Flying is fun and one of the greatest experiences of life. Of that there can be no doubt. At the same time it calls for a very high degree of self-discipline and consideration for others. This is known as airmanship. It does not mean being 'stuffy' and humorless, but it means thorough preparation, meticulous checking, careful planning, practice, and, above all, knowing one's own limitations. There is no place for cowboys in the sky. Remembering that – go flying.

Robert Pooley
Master of the Guild of Air Pilots
and Air Navigators

Introduction

To be asked to write an introduction to a book such as this is a daunting experience. Very quickly you realize that you are one of the main characters in the book and are being portrayed as others see you. Assuming the role of judge and jury, I must hastily conclude that the good bits about me should be inscribed on tablets of stone, while the less favourable parts are due entirely to inaccurate reporting.

But this is a book about learning to fly, and part of the scenario is the role of the flying instructor and the material he has to work with. Flying instructors are an odd bunch of people. They can fly aeroplanes, probably better than most people, so why do they not go on and fly bigger aircraft, advance in their chosen profession, instead of sticking in the rut of teaching people to fly?

It's difficult to define, so perhaps a brief anecdote will make things clearer. It concerns an occasion during my service in Jordan in the early 50s. At that time no Ordnance Survey had been made of the country, and so no detailed maps were available. All you had was a sheet of paper with a few place-names marked on it, vaguely in the correct places, and in between were the words 'Rock' and 'Sand', with further variations of 'Sand' and 'Rock'. Part of my function was to be able to fly to places within the country at the drop of a hat so I decided the only thing was to get to know the country intimately, map or no map. Thus I spent days flying in a light aircraft getting to know landmarks and generally becoming familiar with the various landscapes.

Now, wherever you went in Jordan, no matter how remote the place, you would find a Bedouin tent with a family and their camels and goats. One day we were over a very bleak, inhospitable bit of desert, and below was a solitary Bedouin tent. In the aircraft with me was a Jordanian pilot, to whom I said: 'Let's land and have a word with the people.' So down we went. In the desert the surface is quite suitable for small aircraft, and it was no problem to land beside the tent and taxi up to their front door. Nobody showed surprise at our arrival, and within minutes we were offered the inevitable coffee. After the statutory time of talking about nothing, the conversation went something like this.

Me: 'What is the name of this district?'

Bedouin: 'I don't know.'

Me: 'Then what is the name of this place?'

Bedouin: 'I don't know.'

In an effort to evoke some mutual sympathy and perhaps stimulate further discussion on the local geography, I said:

'You must be like us, you are lost.'

To which he replied, 'I'm not lost. I'm not going anywhere.'

So perhaps flying instructors are not lacking a sense of direction. They are not lost. This is simply what they want to do.

Then there is the other half of the equation – the student, the raw material the instructor has to mould into an aircraft captain. Can you generalize about students? No, because each is an individual displaying traits, foibles, discrepancies, idiosyncrasies, strengths of character, weaknesses of character – just everything that makes up a mortal being. Some even eat garlic for breakfast! Is there a difference between those who want to fly military training aircraft and those who want to fly the civilian puddle-jumpers? Again no; only the environment is different.

In the services you start with a certain number on a course and, by a process of elimination, you finally hone them down to that wonderful stage where only the best have survived. Elimination is a harsh process. There is no appeal against being assessed as a danger to yourself and a menace to others.

With the civilian student pilot, the one controlling factor is money. Flying is quite expensive, so without the financial wherewithal there is an abrupt termination to the effort.

Given the necessary cash, student pilots of the civilian breed can be categorized as follows. The first is the person who wants to be taught flying because he has an end-product for the skill he will acquire, be it as a professional pilot or for everyday private business. The second is the person who simply must learn to fly. With them there is an inner urge that cannot be satisfied except by getting into the air. Once this type is committed to the air, nothing will keep them on the ground. The third category is the character who wants to learn to fly only so that he can impress his girlfriend. They have the money, and in this hard commercial world one has still to eat bread.

The writer of this book comes into the second category. Submerged, just below the surface, has lurked for years a secret, silent, frustrated aviator. Like him, many have had to labour for years to accumulate the financial background to enable them to indulge in a *divertissement* that can never amount to more than a hobby. It was never intended to be capable of paying the rent, the butcher and the baker. But their enthusiasm for this new-found, or long-awaited, outlet is something to admire and applaud. Every waking minute of every fleeting hour, when they are not engaged in thinking about those things that earn salaries, are spent dreaming, self-analysing, remonstrating for errors committed, self-flagellation for having the audacity even to attempt this all-absorbing pursuit.

Pat is fortunate in having Marion, who is, priorities not defined, wife, secretary, second pilot and memory bank for all matters aeronautical. Marion has never done a bad landing but, I am sure, she has had to accept responsibility for quite a few. If not the total responsibility, at least the odium of having to listen to the post mortem on why they happened.

But this much is good. Here we have a man who has the ability to put into words the aspirations, the joys, the difficulties, the human failings, the things that go through a person's mind, while they are being taught to fly. The book is not only highly readable: it is a revelation of what is endured during the first tentative essays into this new dimension – the air.

Many occasions will, and do, occur when a student will (by his actions or reactions, his over-confidence or lack of application) find himself in a modicum of difficulty. He will be up there when he wished he was down here. When you get into difficulty on the ground, you can stop, but in the air you must keep going.

An old airline captain was once asked to sum up the art of flying in a few words. He said: Ninety-five per cent of the time I am bored. The other five per cent I am just plain scared.'

Still we go on flying and will go on flying. It is a way of life, a means of transport and a subject we shall never tire of talking about.

Wing Commander Jock Dalgleish OBE

Acknowledgements

To the best of my belief, this book is honest, decent, truthful . . . and accurate. Since it is a personal account of the ups and downs of learning to fly, any errors, omissions or plain, straightforward carelessnesses are mine wholly and solely.

However, I am duty bound to thank a number of people for their assistance. Indeed, without their help, neither I nor this book would ever have got off the ground.

First, thanks are due to my flying instructor, Jock Dalgleish, for his fortitude in the face of some unparalleled stupidities both on the ground and in the air.

To Jim Nisbet, for always making himself available to answer patiently the wildest of student-pilot questions and also for double-checking the flying facts contained in this book.

To Mike and Doddy Madden, who supplied the greater proportion of the photography – along with much moral support.

To Dave Berrie, now flying commercially, who in the early days often went out of his way to give me practical experience – especially about what to do when lost!

To Tom, Mitch and Andy, scholars and gentlemen of ATC – the voices of a truth forever on the scaffold.

And to all surviving members of the famous Red Sparrows Formation Flying Team, and fellow aviators in the Class of '83.

Prologue

There are literally dozens of books about learning to fly: deadly earnest books, highly technical books, tongue-in-cheek books and downright comical books. Some of them are so complicated that they reduce you to tears of frustration in the battle to master them. Others fall over themselves to give you a laugh a page but neglect to provide the sort of detail that would be useful to a student pilot. A few more take themselves so seriously that you begin to wonder why, if flying is so dreadfully sepulchral, anybody bothers to take it up.

As excellent as they may be in their own way, of all those I have read – and I have read many – none prepared me for the real experience of learning to fly. None accurately predicted the wonder, the alarm, the glee, the tension or the satisfaction I would encounter. None took into account the fact that I, like the vast majority of student pilots I have met, am not in the least courageous, a long way from decisive, and distanced by a million miles from anything mildly resembling intelligent. As for the macho image some of them enthusiastically tried to thrust upon me, all I can say is that anyone who regards a motorized vehicle as a virility symbol, or an extension of their bodies, would be wise to consult a psychiatrist – or a good mechanic – forthwith.

Allow me to give you a couple of for-instances to clarify what I mean.

In the early days of studentship, when I would return white-knuckled and jelly-limbed from a particularly vicious spinning exercise to consult a book which told me that spinning an aircraft should hold no terrors, I could do no more than laugh hollowly. Similarly, while carrying out instrument-flying details in dense cloud, when the aircraft seemed to have a will of its own, none of these authors had explained that it is perfectly natural in the early stages for the machine to go anywhere it damn' well pleases; nor that one should accept it and will, eventually, master it.

Most of these books are, of course, written by highly qualified aeronauts who seem unable to make allowances for plain, old-fashioned stupidity or equally straightforward cowardliness. Because they possess neither of these fallibilities, they go on to assume that anyone who takes up flying will not have them either. They certainly make no allowance for those of us who find it difficult to add or subtract without recourse to fingers and who often become hopelessly lost in nothing more geographically complicated than a corridor.

What I have attempted to do here, therefore, is combine the 'what's it really like' element with the mandatory technical element: to produce a single volume that takes you step by step through the physical and mental experiences, in conjunction with the nuts-and-bolts material you must learn.

In which case, you are getting what amounts to two books for the price of one. And that, at least, should start us off on a pretty amicable footing.

The intention of this book, then, is to transmit the happy fact that learning to fly will be the greatest experience you ever had with all your clothes on; and to prove beyond reasonable doubt that it's a lot simpler than might at first be believed.

I hope it will also show that, if I can do it, anybody can do it.

This book is for people who have an urge to fly aeroplanes and who continually promise themselves that one day they'll pin wings on their chests. It's for those ordinary, everyday dreamers who covet the fantasy of being the commander of a flying machine.

What a delicious thought that is. Savour it for a moment; and while you're doing so, consider that in just forty hours from now, you could be there. Conjure up the vision of yourself in the left-hand seat, headset nonchalantly adopted over a well-shaped and rakish peaked cap, and you in total control. Maybe there's even a trimly built lady (or man, depending on your predilection) sitting alongside, who's marvelling at your every authoritative gesture.

Well, you can forget that for a start. If you're anything like most trainee flyers, it will be quite a long time before you are expert enough, or brave enough, to do so much as unglue your eyes from the cockpit instruments – let alone your hands. All in all, you're going to be far too busy even to consider what you have in mind; and in the early days, survival is all you will be thinking about.

But back to those ordinary, everyday people – those who haven't the faintest idea of what the gaining of a Private Pilot's Licence (PPL) entails or what it costs in time, cash and effort. This book is for them.

If you have the staying-power to reach the end, you will find the answers to a lot of questions which (a) your flying instructor will assume you are sensible enough to know already, and will therefore neglect to fill you in on; (b) you are afraid to ask, because he will consider you less than sensible; (c) can't be found in the regular training manuals since – as I've said, those scholarly tomes tend not to take the student's initial trepidation into account, and concentrate on matters technical rather than personal.

This, then, is an account of how I did it. It may not be the way you do it, but it will be generally very similar. In essence, I'm attempting to give you the benefit of my small experience – the joys, the traumas, the euphoria, the wrinkles, the cock-ups, the lot. The technical material has been vetted by one of the finest airmen in the business. The remainder is my own recollection of the supreme thrill of learning to fly.

What qualifies me to assume this stance? Only that I've done it and you haven't. I'm certainly no expert, but even Albert Einstein admitted that the uninformed casual observer could quite often solve problems the informed couldn't. It's a different angle on things, nothing more; but it just might provide the impetus to get you up out of your chair and into the flying seat.

Stand by.

1 So You Want to be a Pilot?

Flying aeroplanes requires three elementary attributes: the desire, a modicum of natural co-ordination, and the basic physiological equipment.

Desire, of course, is in the mind of the hankerer. Whether it's the physical experience of flying that turns you on or the excruciating envy you experience when watching pilots – even birds – going through their aerial paces, is neither here nor there. You don't have to be poetic about it, just eager – that's sufficient.

Next, natural co-ordination. They do say that, if you can drive a car, you can also fly an aeroplane – which is all very reassuring, though if the number of people we liquidate on our roads each year is anything to go by, maybe not being able to drive a car might be a better qualification.

The way I see it is this. If you can walk across a room, sober, without knocking the furniture over, you've got a good chance of becoming a pilot.

Talking of drink, many airmen don't. On the other hand, many do – including this one. It's all a matter of personal inclination, plus the discipline to realize that anyone who climbs into a flying machine with a bigger tankful than the flying machine is going to end up killing himself or, at best, killing someone else. Even more importantly, the Civil Aviation Authority (CAA) will almost certainly revoke your licence if they get downwind of your breath. The rule I adopt is to give alcohol a miss for twenty-four hours before a flight. After the trip, of course, you can become as legless as you wish. And if you fly with me, you'll definitely wish.

MEDICAL REQUIREMENTS

Being completely physically fit is better than not being fit where flying is concerned. Having all the bits and pieces in the right place also helps. It's true to say, however, that the CAA adopts an extremely unprejudiced view where physical disabilities are experienced. Each case is judged on its merits by their medical examiners; and from what I can understand, they'd rather you fly than not, if you see what I mean. Indeed, if you care to search, there are even special flying training establishments for the disabled – and the one set up by the late Sir Douglas Bader is not the least of these.

Will your gender dramatically affect your ability to fly? Not a bit of it. There are good and bad pilots of both sexes. Several female fliers of my acquaintance have no trouble in regularly out-flying their male colleagues. Having said that, I must now apologize to women readers for the use of the male gender throughout this book. Please accept my word that it implies nothing save a desire for consistency.

Before you are allowed to fly solo, it's mandatory that you have a full medical examination. If you're aged between seventeen and forty – seventeen is the minimum age at which you can qualify for a PPL – the medical remains valid for five years. Over forty, but under fifty, you have to renew your medical certificate every two years. Between fifty and seventy, it's an annual visit to the surgery; over seventy, the medical must be taken at six-monthly intervals. The medicals include cardiograms and chest X-rays, though the frequency of these depends largely upon age and standard of general fitness. All pilots, however, are obliged to report to their CAA medical examiner any illness which occurs during the period between medicals.

The doctors conducting the medicals are specially appointed by the CAA, and they are empowered to issue a CAA medical certificate on the spot. Marvellously, the certificate is also your student pilot's licence. So, having gone through the medical, you will walk from the consulting room, clutching that important piece of paper, on what can only be described as cloud nine. You are A1 fit, you are authorized to fly aeroplanes totally unaided, and you are a pilot . . . nearly.

Oddly enough, no proof as to your fit mental state is necessary. Presumably you are weighed up along the way by the medico, your instructor and other club members; and should you show any tendencies towards suicide or genocide, maybe someone will catch on and point it out. But on thinking about it, I conclude that it's really unimportant – most of the flyers I know are not all there anyway.

Notwithstanding that, you certainly will require a little nous – like knowing your left from your right. Like realizing that if you are flying at 1,500 feet and there's a hill in front of you with an established height of 2,000 feet, you will have to elevate yourself somewhat or you'll not be watching *Match of the Day* come the weekend. Like being able to do simple arithmetic in your head and simple fractions on paper.

WRITTEN EXAMS

You'll need these skills because you will be required to sit four written examinations before you receive that Private Pilot's Licence. The four subjects are: 1. Airframes and Engines. 2. Navigation. 3. Meteorology. 4. Air Law.

They do, of course, have to be studied for. The terms of licence qualification demand at least fifteen hours ground-school training, though all the student pilots I've ever met have completed it with no trouble whatsoever and have subsequently taken the exams in their stride. After all, at this stage you're not hankering to fly 747s: you simply want to know how to get a light aircraft off the ground, and down again, without decorating the surrounding scenery with small bits of it. Thus a level of practical and theoretical competence that keeps you and everybody else safe is the thing to aim for. Your instructor is the final arbiter of that, and he certainly won't let you up into the air on your own until he's completely confident of getting his aeroplane back in approximately the same shape as it left.

The exams, then, are not to be dreaded and, quite reasonably, you won't be told to sit them unless there's a better-than-fair chance of success. The pass-mark for each paper, incidentally, is seventy per cent, and the questions are of the multiple-choice variety. Fortunately, you don't take the exams all of a rush – they're usually spread throughout the training period. Equally fortunately, you can still fly the various solos (circuit and cross-country) whether you have all the exams under your belt or not.

Here's how it works. The purpose of solo cross-country exercises is to give you the opportunity to practise the navigation, air-law, air-frames and engines, and meteorology theory picked up at ground-school classes. On the other hand, the written examinations are part of the training scheme of things and a necessary proof of competence for the Civil Aviation Authority. So, in essence, if your instructor assesses you as having absorbed enough knowledge to make solo forays safely, he will send you solo; but always within the CAA guidelines that ground training must support flying, and vice versa. For advancement's sake, therefore, you will take the trouble to stack up a pretty comprehensive understanding of all the subjects mentioned as an incentive for your instructor to allow you to go it alone.

AIR SAFETY

In the relatively short time I've been flying, literally dozens of people have questioned not only my ability to aviate but also my sanity for wanting to. It seems that even in this modern day, with excellently engineered and expertly maintained aircraft, flying is still considered a dangerous practice. In truth, if there is a hazard involved, it's the human rather than the mechanical element that puts it there. Complacency causes accidents; carelessness causes accidents; pride causes accidents. So far as I know, no aircraft has yet been proved to have any of these characteristics.

For what it's worth, here's a piece of advice from someone who, without fail, has made every error in the aviation book. Before you move that aeroplane one single inch, check everything that's checkable . . . then check it again . . . and again. Furthermore, never ever consider yourself above asking for help. The way I understand it, the first deadly sin has accounted for more problems in the air than just about anything.

The newcomer to flying will be agreeably impressed by the rigorous safety procedures and drills one must adhere to in all flying activities. These begin well before you enter the aircraft, and they don't finish until some several minutes after you get out.

What's more, there exists a particularly strict law of the air, every statute of which must be obeyed to the letter. It all makes a great deal of sense, and it ensures the highest possible standards of airmanship.

So my reply to those people who question air safety is this. How often, when you jump into your car, do you check tyres, brakes, hydraulics, battery-charging, fuel, oil, mixture, radio, instruments and bodywork? The fact is, you have to do all that, and more, with an aeroplane. Every trip.

I'll be discussing safety procedures at appropriate points throughout the book. Basically, however, all you have to do is get the principles and processes of safety firmly implanted in your mind (there are simple mnemonics to aid memory in this area), and then, even if you're as shatter-pated as I am, you'll be as safe as houses.

Finally, the misinformed will insist on telling me that landing an aircraft is the trickiest part of the flying operation. They will very likely try to tell you the same. Don't listen, because it's a fallacy. A touchdown holds no more terrors for the able pilot than parking the average family car. In fact, it's a lot easier, since, for a start, there are unlikely to be any other vehicles in the immediate vicinity of where you want to arrive on the runway. So the only thing you can hit is the tarmac. And if you carry out all the checks, adopt the correct approach angle and maintain the right speed for the job, you'll reach an acme in pleasure peaks that all the advanced driving techniques in the world could never surpass.

That's always supposing the club wag doesn't buttonhole you before your first solo landing with the old adage: 'There are three types of landing, Sidney. One you taxi away from. One you walk away from. And one they carry you away from!'

The choice, however, need never be made.

While you're digesting that, may I point you in the direction of a useful little publication called *CAP 53. The Private Pilot's Licence: A Guide to licensing and rating requirements.* It's published by the Civil Aviation Authority. At the time of writing it costs less than two quid, and it tells you everything you need to know about gaining your licence – the medical qualifications, the age restrictions, the exams, the training required. You can order it direct from the CAA at Grenville House, Cheltenham, Gloucestershire. Telephone: (0242) 35151.

SUMMARY

Analysis of PPL Flying Requirements

A minimum of forty hours flying instruction, conducted in accordance with a recognized syllabus, must be logged in order to qualify for a PPL.

A minimum of twenty hours shall be as dual instruction including:

1. A minimum of fours hours instruction in instrument flying.
2. At least four hours in pilot navigation.
3. No fewer than two hours stall spin awareness and avoidance training.

A minimum of ten hours as pilot-in-command, i.e. solo including:

1. At least four hours cross-country flights. Within that four hours the syllabus also includes a solo qualifying cross-country flight. This requires two intermediate landings, one of which must be at least fifty nautical miles from the departure aerodrome.

The final handling test monitored by a CAA examiner. (One hour.)

In addition, there is a navigation flight test (NFT) – which includes: flight-planning, in-flight log-keeping ATC liaison, map-reading, course-keeping and certain simulated exercises, e.g. diversion following bad weather conditions.

Ground-School Syllabus

Ground training is an integral part of the recognized syllabus and covers the following subjects: Navigation; Airframes and Engines; Air Law; Meteorology.

Medical Requirements

To keep your licence (student or full PPL) valid, you must undertake a periodic medical examination to gain a Class 111 Medical Certificate, which is part of your licence document. The requirements, according to age and duration, are:

Age	*Validity*
Student/Private Pilot aged 17 to under 40	60 months
Student/Private Pilot aged 40 to 50	24 months
Student/Private Pilot aged 50 to 70	12 months
Student/Private Pilot aged over 70	6 months

Under the rules of the Air Navigation Order, licence-holders must notify the CAA Medical Department of any incapacitating injury or sickness absence of twenty consecutive days or more. Confirmation of pregnancy is also necessary.

Student pilots must not carry passengers unless accompanied by a qualified flying instructor.

Every qualified private pilot is expected to hold a Flight Radiotelephony Operator's Licence.

The examination to qualify for the above is not difficult and may be conducted by your Chief Flying Instructor. It pays to get an r/t licence, otherwise you will be infringing CAA rules; and for what it costs, it's easy to be 'legal'.

2 The Club

Rightly and properly, I suppose, when an individual approaches middle age those youthful dreams of becoming a pilot should have gone the way of all childish toys. Yet however hard many of us try, a few formative ambitions tend to get lodged and linger on. It's the sort of subconscious juvenility which forces grown men to set up an intricate model railway layout in the attic and never let a child near it.

It follows, then, that while I may never have given even a passing thought in the last thirty years to that most voluptuous of 50s celluloid sweethearts, Piper Laurie, I have most certainly pondered the equally classic lines of Piper Tri-Pacer.

The fact is, I was a youngster at a time when Adolf Hitler was doing his damnedest to blast us all out of existence and when young men with huge handlebar moustaches and admirable aplomb were closing him down. As far as I was concerned – and I must have been all of five – anybody in Air Force blue was somebody to be very close to and, if you were extremely lucky, to have your hair ruffled by.

That's the principle of my dream – what's yours? And let me tell you, once you have the motivation, nothing should stop you fulfilling the aspiration. Money? Forget it – divorce the spouse and sell the house. Time? Listen, you never liked work anyway. Availability of a flying club? Ah, well, now this could be serious, indeed.

FLYERS ARE DEMOCRATS

The Yellow Pages will give you the address of your local flying club. Failing that, get in touch with the magazine *Pilot* (see p. 34). They have a back issue that lists just about every club in the country.

There are, by all accounts, a pretty diverse range of clubs

throughout the UK. Some have superb ground-training facilities and average instructors. Some have quite brilliant instructors and a paucity of facilities. And some have varying proportions of both.

In theory, it really doesn't matter, because when all is boiled down, it's only your contribution and your application to the task that are relevant. In practice, everything depends on what you want out of life in general and your flying membership in particular. Personally, I chose the club which, in my considered opinion, had the two most important ingredients for my money: a red-hot Chief Flying Instructor . . . and a members' bar. Had it been possible, that red-hot instructor would also have been bribable and the bar entirely free. No such luck, needless to say.

Flying clubs, or flying schools if you wish, are bound by a fairly rigid constitution which determines membership privileges and so on. In this respect, they are no different from any other type of club in the land. But unlike quite a few of the elitist institutions (golf clubs, country clubs, etc), the flying versions are generally more democratic.

For instance, race, colour and creed don't enter into it. Neither does sponsorship, blackballing or any of the other discriminatory measures designed to keep 'undesirables' out. In the normal course of events, all you need do is ask to join – or take an air-experience flight – and I can very nearly guarantee that they will bite your hand off. Flying may be thought of as a rich man's sport, and there are, indeed, very many rich men following it, but these are far outnumbered by ordinary, overdrawn, mortgaged-to-the-hilt Janets and Johns. All in all, I think I can say, without inviting too much argument, that flying-training establishments rarely refuse membership to anyone brandishing negotiable currency.

LIVING WITH YOUR INSTRUCTOR

Now a word about the person who counts the most in the learning-to-fly scheme of things – your instructor.

A flying instructor, and particularly the one who eventually adopts you, is about the closest you'll ever get to God while still inhabiting this world. You will come to learn that, unlike ordinary people, who are blessed with only the average amount of ability, your flying instructor has two of everything. He has double the brainpower, double the initiative and double the acumen of normal mortals.

From this you will realize how important it is to get off on the right foot with the man who is going to teach you everything he knows – or, more properly, everything he thinks you can absorb. Not only that: he is going to waste a lot of valuable time on your behalf – time which he could more profitably spend in snooker halls or betting shops. Treat him with the greatest deference, therefore, and you'll do fine. A little grovelling certainly won't go amiss.

As a breed, flying instructors are a happy band, and they are generally endowed with a fine sense of humour and a keen sense of the ridiculous. They have to be that way, otherwise in a very short time they'd be bouncing off rubber walls. This is because students, by and large, are a pretty thick bunch. You don't, as a habit, have to watch a student inadvertently switching off the fuel during a take-off run to realize that, if you don't laugh at it, the nervous breakdown is only a whit away.

From time to time during training, you will notice your instructor turning white. This, as you'll appreciate, is not a terribly good sign. His pallidity, however, won't be induced by fear, because there is nothing you can do to an aeroplane that he hasn't already seen; and it certainly won't be through anger, for instructors rarely lose their cool. On the contrary, he will turn white from the sheer disbelief that you could perpetrate so many errors in so short a space of time. But don't let it play on your mind: it happens to everybody.

Notwithstanding the above, if during your endeavours you happen to notice his eyes glazing over and his lower lip trembling, then is the time to consider whether you have turned him right over the edge and wonder whether he is a fit person to be flying with. At that point, you may wish to begin composing your statement for the subsequent court of enquiry, or decide to conduct all future flights solo.

It's been my experience that instructors tend to impart their knowledge on a need-to-know basis. What this means is that in the early stages they keep you in relative ignorance of how the plane flies, and of how the lump of engine machinery at the front works. It may occur to you, therefore, to find these things out for yourself. The reasons behind your instructor's slowness in divulging all is quite simple. He realizes that, once you get to grips with it, he becomes largely redundant.

It follows then, that the worst thing you can possibly do to your mentor is make him feel unwanted. Given the situation where you announce that you have reached such a level of competence that his presence is now only a token one to satisfy the air-law legislation, he will almost certainly prove differently. Like by taking the plane up to 3,000 feet, putting it into a pernicious spin and then asking what you propose doing about it. That is called power. Be warned: flying instructors wield power with a conviction that would make Attila the Hun look positively timorous.

All of that aside, the need-to-know hypothesis is an eminently sensible one. It prevents your mind becoming cluttered, in the early days, with information you don't really need at that stage. It obviates a lot of confusion, too. So you'll discover that the necessary detail sticks more readily when it's drip-fed to you at every successive lesson; and as you build your hours, you will also build your knowledge. You'd better get it clear at the start, too, that you will never know all that your instructor knows. Neither will you be able to fly with his consummate skill. It's a pretty good idea to tell him so from time to time, too. He's only human after all, and he needs approbation just as much as you do.

To recap, then, the real secret of learning to fly is also to learn how to be a devout crawler. Take my word for it.

YOUR FELLOW AVIATORS

All in all, the club you join will be basically similar to any other club, in that you'll be surrounded by beginners and experts alike. Many of the latter, you will discover, have been flying since flying began. These people are mines of information and well worth cultivating. Amazingly, too, they rarely treat the learner the way experts in other fields treat learners – with out-and-out disdain. You'll find them only too happy to fill the gaps in your knowledge; and even if you do have only an hour or two flying experience, they'll make you feel you've been at it for years. I put it down to the fact that learning to fly – and making the first solo in particular – is such a graphic experience that their memory of it is still vivid and they realize full well what you are going through.

Be cute, push a few pints in the right direction, and you'll be very surprised at the kind and understanding response you get. What is also quite important is your attitude to fellow students. If your club runs true to form, the people in it will be as diverse a bunch as any you are likely to find. They'll be plumbers, lawyers, cab-drivers, computer programmers, and they'll be of every creed and persuasion. As the months go by, you will learn from them, as they will learn from you.

And always remember: you are not in competition with any of them. Your fellow students will be in various stages of flying training; some will be more advanced than you, some won't. Also, some will be natural pilots who make your performance look pretty ham-fisted by comparison. It doesn't matter – the way you make out is the only thing that counts. And even if the bloke who started after you gets to solo first, it shouldn't follow that you have to go all out to try to beat him to the end of the course.

AIRCRAFT TYPES

What about the aircraft you'll be flying? Invariably, they'll be unsophisticated basic trainers which are designed to forgive errors and incompetence. Many have the inbuilt characteristic that allows you to fly 'hands off' when in a bind, and the plane will get itself out of trouble. Some of them, in fact, give you the distinct impression that you are merely along for the ride.

I've flown a variety of different types and, for what it's worth, I believe there's no aircraft to match the Cessna marque of trainers – the 150s, 152s and 172s. They are, in a word, the cream of the aircraft manufacturers' crop; and I'm talking about design rather than price. You might say that they are the Fords of the air, solid, sound, reliable, with all the wrinkles ironed out over many years of adhering to the same basic design ideas. As it happens, I also prefer the handling characteristics of high-wing aircraft, which all the above models are. They're certainly less inclined to 'bad habits' than low-wing types and are definitely easier to fly from the beginner's point of view.

In order to be sure that we both know what I'm talking about, a high-wing aircraft is best described as having wings which sit atop the cockpit, while on low-wing types the wings protrude from the lower fuselage.

Anyway, should the Cessna Aircraft Company happen to read the above *soupçon* of unsolicited testimonial and feel obliged to reciprocate in some manner, they may deliver the new 152 to me anytime they like.

SUMMARY

Notes on Choosing Your Flying Club

Flying-training clubs vary greatly in their range of aircraft available, training facilities and social opportunities. Fees also differ from outfit to outfit.

When choosing a club, your major concern should be to discover whether it has the professionalism to put you through the course in the shortest possible time.

Now the forty-three hours flying time needed for a PPL is a *minimum* requirement, and not everyone has the aptitude to get through in that time. Nevertheless, a good club will do its damnedest to turn you into a pilot as quickly as possible. I am aware that one or two notorious clubs will keep you bashing up the hours more out of a desire for revenue than to give you the necessary experience. There are pirates everywhere, and as with everything else it's a case of 'buyer beware'.

In addition, for workload reasons, some clubs make a habit of switching flying instructors on you – one week you get Mr X, the next it's Miss Y, and so on. Such treatment can be very frustrating, since you are never able to establish a relationship with an individual instructor; and this is not much use in a situation where continuous assessment of your progress determines how speedily you qualify for your licence.

In that case, immediately you have taken your initial

air-experience flight, and an instructor has weighed up your potential, make it clear that you expect to qualify within the statutory number of hours. Similarly, insist that your training be conducted by him and him alone. If he replies that he is only an assistant instructor and cannot see you through the entire course, put the same points to the chief flying instructor. Given that you have average potential, you should hope for a loose affirmation of the first point and a firm promise on the second.

These days, many clubs make use of computer-controlled flight-simulators, as well as other items of micro-electronic gadgetry. They are very fine in their own way, but always bear in mind that nothing – and I mean nothing – can ever take the place of solid flying experience.

Flying Clubs in the UK

For a comprehensive list of UK clubs, contact *Pilot* magazine at 88 Burlington Road, New Malden, Surrey KT3 4NT. Editor: James Gilbert.

Flying Instructor Ratings

People contemplating flying training often wonder to whom they are entrusting their safety – not to mention their money. The following is a run-down of the basic qualifications instructors are obliged to possess in order to operate in a teaching capacity.

AFI: *Assistant Flying Instructor*
- (i) Must have held a PPL for not less than twelve months;
- (ii) A minimum of 150 hours as pilot-in-command;
- (iii) An Instrument Meteorological Conditions rating;

QFI: *Qualified Flying Instructor*
- (i) Should have logged no fewer than 400 hours as pilot-in-command;
- (ii) A minimum of 200 hours instruction experience;
- (iii) Over twenty hours cross-country flying experience as pilot-in-command.

(iv) One of the above cross-country flights must be of no fewer than 300 miles duration.

CFI: *Chief Flying Instructor*

(i) A QFI may become the Chief Flying Instructor of a club as and when a vacancy occurs.

(ii) To qualify as a CAA examiner, a QFI should have logged no fewer than 1,500 hours of instruction.

Basic Flying Training Equipment

The following is a rough list of the equipment you will eventually require to function properly as a student pilot.

1. Pilot's log book.
2. Maps (air charts) of the area in which you will be operating. These are to a scale of 1:500,000 and 1:250,000.
3. Knee-pad. This is a small clipboard with an elasticated strap which is worn on the lower thigh when flying. It is invaluable for taking notes while keeping one hand free.
4. Scale ruler and chinagraph pencil.
5. Navigator's square protractor.
6. Navigator's computer – a kind of circular slide-rule for making rapid computations.

Your club is sure to have supplies of all this material, and they will probably sell it to you at preferential rates. So buy nothing until you've made cost comparisons.

3 Air Experience

Exactly what does it feel like to steer an aircraft in flight for the very first time? Better still, what kind of thrill do you get when you first haul back on the yoke and feel that graceful bird unstick from the runway?

I suppose the experience hits different people differently. But do you remember the day, after all those grazed knees, when you mastered the bike? It's like that. And do you remember going out on your first date? It's like that. Do you remember, also, your introduction to ice-cream? It's like that.

It's every great sensation you ever had, plus some you didn't, all rolled into one: blancmange with the coloured bits on top; a brand-new Alfa Romeo at the front door; the Littlewoods man with good news; the engagement party; a salary increase. You name it and that's just the way it is. For years, I wondered what Ernest Hemingway was on about with his moment of truth. Now I know.

For a more down-to-earth and more constructive description, maybe I should tell you what happened the first time I helped an aircraft become airborne. Moreover, it may help if you know exactly what was physically happening to the plane and, additionally, what was going on in my mind.

THE PRINCIPLES OF FLIGHT

Those of you who already know what makes an aircraft fly may care to skip this bit, but be warned, there will be questions about it in your CAA exams. So it will pay to read it up somewhere – and in a great deal more depth than given here.

Like all reasonably-put-together planes, the one I first flew had, working fore to aft, an engine of 100 hp capacity, a set of wings or mainplane, a tailplane with elevators, and a fin complete with rudder. This arrangement produces thrust via the engine, lift from the wings, longitudinal stability via the tail, and directional stability from the fin.

From this it can be reasoned that the four forces involved in flight are lift, gravity, thrust and drag. And when all four forces are equalized, you are, in every sense, flying.

Now let's understand how these forces are created, or overcome, to reach that desirable state of affairs called flight.

Cut a section through the wing of a plane and you'll see a configuration rather like an elongated golf wood. It's called an aerofoil and happens to be the very shape which gives you the lift you need.

Force the wing through air by means of an internal combustion engine, for instance, and the flow of air across the top of the aerofoil will act differently from the airflow beneath. In essence, because of the curved shape of the wing's leading edge, air is made to travel faster over the top than it does underneath. Now, a law of physics states that when a fluid (which is what air is, if you think about it) is made to behave in this way, the increase in speed is followed smartly by a drop in pressure. Therefore the pressure on the wing's upper surface drops dramatically while, below, the pressure remains constant.

It doesn't now take too much imagination to see that if the wing were to be tilted at a slight angle to the airflow, the air

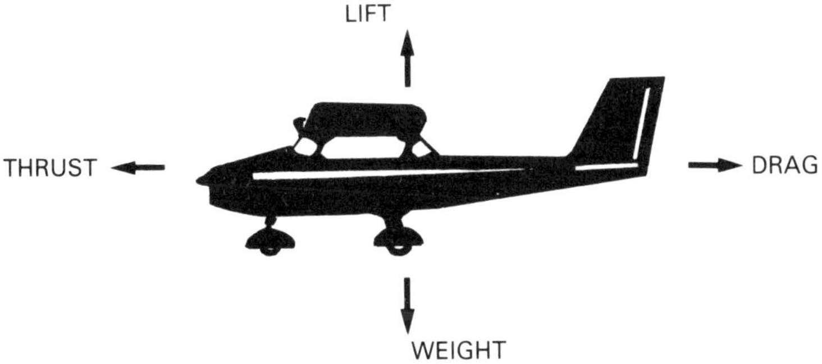

Fig. 1. When all four forces are equalized, you are, in every sense, flying

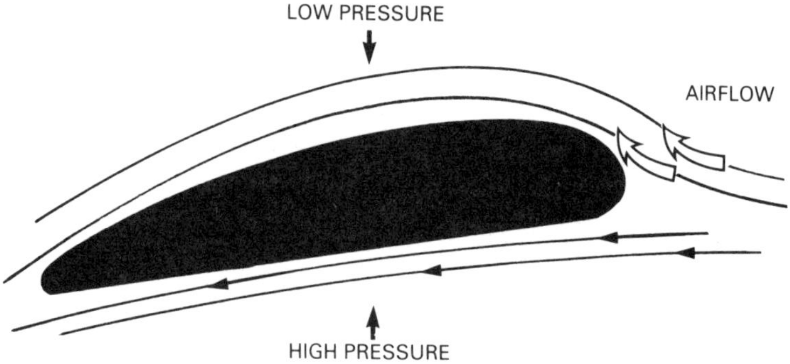

Fig. 2. The air flows faster across the top of the aerofoil, causing the pressure to drop. The pressure beneath remains constant until we increase the angle of attack. Now pressure increases and lift is generated

would move faster over the top and pressure would decrease rapidly. Conversely, the pressure beneath the wing increases, and the lifting force is thereby generated.

So lift can be controlled either by making the airflow faster or by increasing the wing's angle of attack in relation to that airflow. That makes sense.

One final point worth remembering about all of this is that lift is measured from a point known as the centre of pressure. The only reason you'll want to know that is because the centre of pressure alters as the angle of attack alters. When you perform your induced-stall flying exercises, you will experience the effect of this. By decreasing your forward speed and by pulling the nose of the aircraft up so that the wings are at such an angle of attack that a no-lift situation exists, you are imminent to a stall. What happens is that the obtuse angle of attack creates drag; you have little or no forward speed and thus little or no airflow; so the centre of pressure moves forward towards the leading edge of the wing and eventually the lift breaks down. You are then effectively in control – or rather, only just in control of what will shortly be a flying brick.

More about stalling exercises in a nonce. Meanwhile, back at the aircraft.

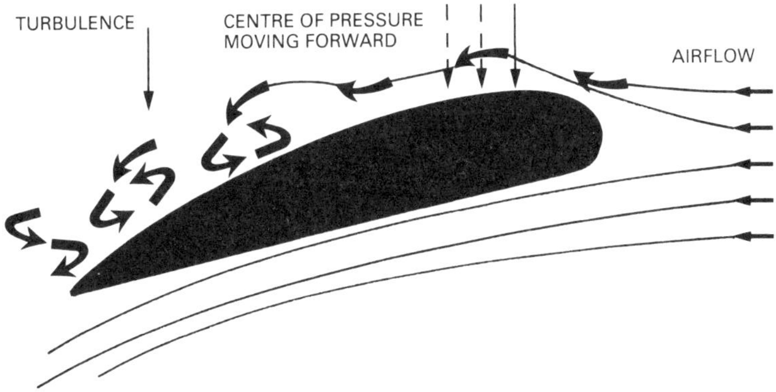

Fig. 3. Characteristics of a stall

The machine you fly will have certain control surfaces. There are

(a) ailerons to control the aircraft in the rolling plane, i.e. for banking and turning;
(b) flaps to increase lift in certain take-off and landing conditions;
(c) a rudder, for controlling yaw – that's nose to the left or right;
(d) the elevators for nose up, nose down and level flight.

You will probably also find a device called a trim tab hinged to the trailing edge of the elevators. This does exactly what its name implies by providing small adjustments to the pitch of the aircraft, taking pressure off the control column, and making your flying life that much easier.

So now we know what gets us into the air, and what helps steer our course once we're up there.

The controls for all of this are simple enough to understand. Inside the cockpit you have a 'stick' or a wheel which operates the ailerons and the elevators, and you have a set of foot-pedals for rudder operation. The flaps are operated by a lever, and the trim-tab works by rotating a notched wheel.

The foregoing is much more than you need know for your first flying lesson – or, as they call it, your air-experience flight. Even so, it's a pretty good idea to have it installed in your mind and shouldn't be in any way harmful.

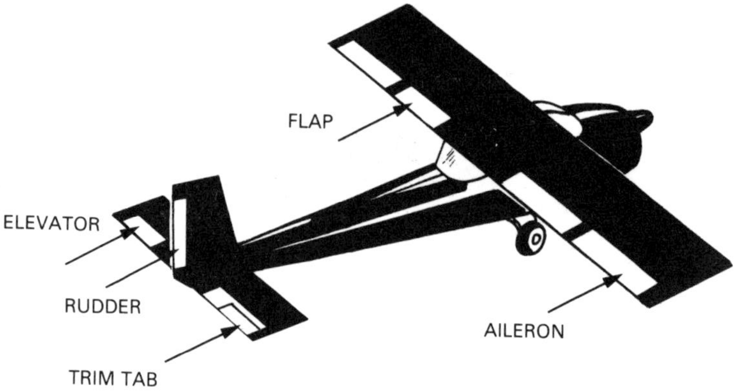

Fig. 4. Control surfaces

'CLIMB ABOARD!'

My air-experience flight came about on a fairly blustery Sunday morning in April. The wind was gusting 20 knots (that's 23 mph on account of 33 knots equals 38 mph – so the simple equation is $20/33 \times 38/1 = 23$) and the sky was overcast, with stratus at an altitude of some 2,500 feet.

I arrived at Turnhouse Flying Club at the due time, having been given this thirty-minute trip by my daughters as a birthday gift. (Hereinafter known as 'silly half-hour'.) Inside, a man in his early sixties was hoovering the carpet – there was nobody else about. I gave him my name and nature of my business.

'Oh, very good,' he said. 'Take a seat for a moment.' And he continued hoovering.

I picked up a *Pilot* magazine from the table and flipped through it idly, all the while pondering the fact that it wasn't much of a club that left the janitor in charge when paying customers had an appointment. After a while, the hoovering stopped and the janitor gave me a printed waiver form to complete. In effect it told me to put my signature to the news that Turnhouse Flying Club took no responsibility for any loss or damage I might incur from that moment on.

As I filled in the form, I made idle conversation with the man. One question I put was: 'Do you do any flying yourself?'

He looked puzzled for a moment, then said, 'As a matter of fact, I do all the flying around here. You can call me Jock.'

Jock, in the event, turned out to be Wing Commander Jock Dalgleish OBE – ex-wartime Spitfire pilot, and the man who taught HM King Hussein of Jordan to fly. (No wonder the King wears those wings so proudly.) He took his first flight with someone from the Alan Cobham Flying Circus in the 1920s, and rumour has it that he hasn't had his feet on the ground for more than two consecutive days ever since.

'All right, then – let's get you into the *luft*,' he said. 'Not much of a day, I'm afraid. But perfectly satisfactory for our purposes.' Which was pretty high-falutin language for a janitor.

As we walked out to the aircraft parking apron, he filled me in with various bits of information about the aircraft – roughly along the lines I've given you in the previous chapter.

The plane itself was a Cessna 150 – a high-wing monoplane, *circa* 1974, with a tricycle undercarriage. I had yet to realize it but this was the aircraft which would forgive all my mistakes in the following months; this was the bird which would allow me to solo.

For those of you who blenched at the age of the aircraft, I should explain that, unlike the average car, many flying machines are built to last. For a start, they are constructed mainly from aluminium – which doesn't have anywhere near the same rusting qualities as mild steel. Second, the airframes have to be monitored on a regular basis by CAA-approved engineers. Third, aero-engines have both a pre-ordained and a much-documented life. This means that the engine is mandatorily renewed after a given number of flying hours; and during its working life it is subjected to regular inspections and overhauls. Fourth, only a specially licensed aero-engineer is permitted to carry out those inspections and overhauls. Fifth, if any of the inspection provisions is not met, the aircraft is compulsorily grounded.

In these terms, a 1974 aircraft should be as mechanically and structurally sound as a 1987 aircraft. Indeed, to drive the point home, there are a good few 1940s/50s aircraft still scudding around the skies, making aviation history and making some of the newer types look sick.

'Climb aboard and strap in,' ordered Jock. I made towards the co-pilot's seat – the right-hand side of the plane – but Jock indicated the commander's seat. 'No, I want you in that side. This isn't a pleasure trip,' he said ominously. 'Get comfortable while I make an inspection and do a bit of maintenance.'

With which remark he made a thorough job of emptying the cockpit ashtrays. On the subject of ashtrays, it's a sensible notion to keep the contents low and their lids tightly closed, since a semi-inverted entry to a spin will cover the cockpit in flying fag-ends and ash and cover the trainee pilot in confusion.

The cockpit of the 150, as I strapped in, seemed uncomfortably small – allowing about as much elbow-room as the smallest sports car. The safety harness was a perplexity of straps which turned out to be rigid shoulder and lap restraints. None of your inertia reels here. Making the necessary strap adjustments took quite some time, although my trembling fingers weren't contributing anything to the problem. This was to be my first light-plane trip for a long time and, while I desperately wanted to accomplish it, I desperately didn't either.

Eventually I managed to arrange things so that I was both firmly confined and also able to manipulate the rudder pedals and control column comfortably. I've found this operation a deal simpler to accomplish since, but the importance of getting it right before take-off cannot be overstressed. Trying to make re-adjustments in the air is not only undesirable: it's nigh-on impossible.

There now followed a largely perplexing dialogue of instructions on how to start the engine and what to look for *vis-à-vis* the cockpit instruments once it had. These procedures, or vital actions, are the most important you'll ever undertake, because a low fuel level overlooked or a degraded oil pressure missed could well result in a premature and unnecessary obituary in the local paper with your name on it!

INSTRUMENT CHECK

Given the importance of an instrument check before rolling from the apron, it might be an idea right now to show you what you'll be looking at and what you're looking for.

Immediately in front of the co-pilot's seat, i.e. the right-hand seat, in most light aircraft is a bank of instruments which includes fuel-oil pressure, oil temperature, ammeter and air-suction gauges. The first three speak for themselves; and you simply check that you have enough fuel for the exercise, a high oil pressure and a low oil temperature. If that seems rather basic and an insult to your intelligence, you may care to consider that pilots have, in the past, taken off with empty tanks and nil oil pressure, and they doubtless still bear the scars to prove it.

Every pilot is obliged to check his fuel tanks before take-off. He then assesses whether the amount of fuel available is sufficient for the flight, bearing in mind the hourly fuel consumption at cruising speed of the aircraft in question. It's easily worked out. Let's say you are due to travel a distance of 120 miles. Your aircraft cruises at 80 mph and consumes 5 gallons of fuel per hour. The equation, therefore, is:

$$\frac{5 \text{ gallons per hour}}{80 \text{ mph}} \times \frac{120 \text{ miles to travel}}{1} = 7\tfrac{1}{2} \text{ gallons}$$

This same equation would be used in flight to determine fuel remaining in relation to the distance left to run, or where adverse weather conditions force you to consider diverting to a different destination airfield.

The fourth instrument, the ammeter, gives you a reading which shows that the battery is being charged and that the alternator is generating enough electricity to operate navigation lights, flaps, radio and so on. Lastly, the air-suction guage. This shows that the vacuum pump is drawing air in enough quantity to drive the aircraft's gyro-operated instruments.

Now let's take a look at the dial bank on the captain's side of the cockpit. Top left is the airspeed indicator which gives you your speed through the air (not over the ground – more about that later). Next the artificial horizon, the dial with the model aircraft built in that helps you keep wings straight and level. To the right is the altimeter for assessing height. Below these, you'll find a turn and slip indicator which shows the

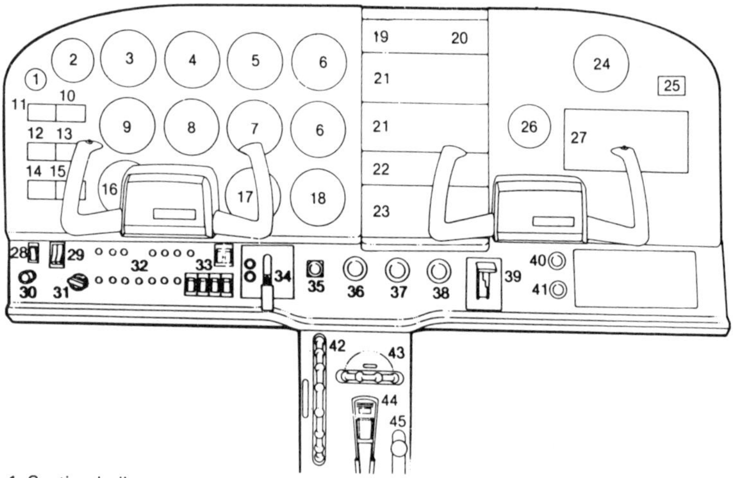

1 Suction Indicator
2 Clock
3 Airspeed Indicator
4 Attitude Indicator
5 Altimeter
6 VHF Navigation Indicator
7 Vertical Speed Indicator
8 Heading Indicator
9 Turn Co-ordinator
10 Fuel Gauge (Right Tank)
11 Fuel Gauge (Left Tank)
12 Ammeter
13 Oil-Pressure Gauge
14 Cylinder Head Temperature Gauge
15 Oil Temperature Gauge
16 Manifold Pressure Gauge
17 Tachometer
18 ADF Radio Navigation Indicator
19 Marker Beacon Indicator
20 Audio Control Panel
21 VHF Communication and Navigation Radio
22 Transponder
23 Autopilot
24 Carburettor Air Temperature Indicator
25 Flight Hour Indicator
26 Exhaust Gas Temperature Gauge
27 ADF Radio
28 Auxiliary Fuel Pump Switch
29 Master Switch
30 Engine Primer
31 Ignition Switch
32 Circuit-Breakers
33 Electrical Switches
34 Landing Gear Lever
35 Carburettor Heat Control
36 Throttle Control
37 Propeller Control
38 Fuel/Air Mixture Control
39 Wing Flaps Control
40 Cabin Heat Control
41 Cabin Air Control
42 Elevator Trim Control
43 Rudder Trim Control
44 Microphone
45 Cowl Flap Control

Fig. 5. Instrument panel of a Cessna Cutlass. A somewhat different layout from a 150, but with essentially the same instrumentation.

degrees of bank and sideslip you put the aircraft into; the direction indicator, a purely mechanical device which is synchronized with a magnetic compass (you'll find the compass located, usually, in the centre of the top windscreen frame), and finally a vertical speed indicator for determining the speed at which the aircraft ascends or descends.

It's worth bearing in mind that the altimeter, the vertical speed and airspeed indicators are pressure instruments and work by sampling air from outside the aircraft via a pitot head, or static vent, while the artificial horizon and direction indicator are operated by gyros. To clarify things, the slip portion of the turn and slip dial works simply by the centrifugal forces generated in a turn – it's nothing more than a marble in a glass tube.

Obviously, the vital actions to be undertaken before releasing the brakes will not immediately sink in. But after a few hours' instruction you'll soon get the drift of it; and even if, in the early days, you make the checks completely in the wrong order, consider it purely academic. Your instructor will put you right every time; and at least you made the effort. Later you'll be more than gratified when the whole process becomes second nature.

Having absorbed all of that, let us return to the Sunday morning in April.

PRE-FLIGHT CHECKS

The very first job on this occasion was to remove the locking device from the control column – it's nothing more than a metal bar device for preventing elevators and ailerons flapping around in a high wind while parked. It is, however, a most important piece of equipment and one to be given undivided attention. I have it on good authority that people have tried taking off with the lock still in place. Of course, they got only as far as the end of the runway, because the control column was immovable. The resulting frantic skid to a halt, or perhaps the smash through the perimeter fence, must have been spectacular in every way.

Second and third jobs: main switches on, a quarter of an inch on the throttle lever, and turn the ignition key.

The engine fairly belted into life, and the vibration within the cockpit was something to behold. Jock then unhooked a microphone from below the instrument panel.

'Edinburgh ground, this is golf-alpha-x-ray-uniform foxtrot. Eastern apron. Request taxi clearance thirty minutes to the south . . . over.'

Fantastic, I thought; and I just couldn't wait to have a go on the blower myself – little realizing that very soon I'd be doing all the radio work and getting into one hell of a verbal mess to boot. The reply that came bellowing from the loudspeaker just above my left ear was a mixture of Cantonese and lower Dutch, or so it seemed; and my inability to understand it set the pattern of near incomprehensibility for the next few months.

An on-going debate exists in my club, and I suspect in many other clubs also, about the advantages of cockpit loudspeakers over headphones – and vice-versa. My preference is for the speaker, perhaps because I was trained on that system, though there are drawbacks with both. For instance, engine noise tends to drown out the cockpit speaker, particularly in a climb at full throttle. On the other hand, while headphones do give a much clearer reception, they somehow isolate the wearer from both engine pitch and the intimacy of direct communication with the instructor.

Really, it's a matter of personal preference – although I'd suggest that the system you begin with should be the one you adhere to throughout.

'Golf-uniform-foxtrot,' came the reply. 'You are cleared to the holding point at two-six. By the northern taxiway. QNH 1025. QFE 1020.'

Jock repeated the bones of this message back to the ground controller so as to assure the latter that we had picked up the instruction correctly. The air-traffic control people are very hot on the precise dissemination and assimilation of messages, as you can imagine – so much so that, if you happen to miss a fact or misinterpret a fact on your readback, they will correct you, and you must repeat it verbatim.

The whole process is an art in itself, demanding the ability to remember a series of unrelated bits of information and then narrate them back. It doesn't take long, however, to cop onto the idea that basic instructions for taxi-ing, take-off and landing come in the same order every time. Thus you know the format of any message for any situation beforehand.

Before we go any farther, let's unravel the message as given.

First, golf-alpha-x-ray-uniform-foxtrot is our registration; you can't miss yours, it's painted in eighteen-inch letters on both sides of the fuselage. You'll notice that the full registration was shortened to just three letters by the controller after communication was established. This is common practice and not only saves time on the airwaves but also prevents tedious, turgid repetition which would soon have everybody comatose.

Second, we were cleared to the holding point of runway two-six. The runway is given that numerical appellation, as you might expect, because it is on a magnetic bearing of 260°, i.e. pointing at and going towards 260°. For the record, all bearings are given in three figures, but runway numbers are quoted in two figures only. Thus: two-six and its reciprocal zero-eight; three-one, one-three etc.

Third, we were told the values of the QNH and QFE operating at that time. These are both evaluations of barometric pressure, and the figures are given in millibars – one millibar equalling thirty feet at sea level. Depending on the type of exercise you are performing, one or other of the figures must be dialled on your altimeter. The QNH, then, is the barometric pressure at airfield level reduced to sea-level.

What it amounts to is this. Once you leave the vicinity of your airfield, the QNH reading on your altimeter will establish your altitude above sea-level – all the better to avoid hills, mountains, TV masts and so on. On the other hand, QFE is the barometric pressure at airfield level. So if you are working around the airport as in, say, a circuits detail, the altimeter will tell you your exact height above the field and will register zero when you land.

For the record, when performing exercises outside a control zone – that's the ten-mile, special-rules radius around every major airfield – you will receive the regional QNH, which is the lowest forecast pressure for that area and to which you must programme your altimeter. You may care to note that the standard altimeter-setting that all the big airline boys adjust to once over 3,000 feet is 1013.2 millibars. Known as the Transition Altitude, it ensures that everyone is on exactly the same setting – so flight-level separation is made safe and easy.

'READY FOR TAKE-OFF'

'Depress the brake pedals to release the brakes,' said Jock. 'Give her a little throttle and taxi out to your left.'

I stamped down on the brake pedals, which are immediately above the rudder pedals. At the same time, I gave the engine some gyp, and the aircraft began, gloriously, to roll. Purely by instinct, I kept my hands off the control column, steering solely on brakes and rudder. Jock was so impressed that he raised an eyebrow.

The plane trundled erratically along the taxiway as I overcompensated on the rudder, each swerve greater than the last, each opposite rudder movement compounding the overall felony.

I learned later that this particular 150 model has a semi-castoring nosewheel. Anyone who has ever attempted to manœuvre a castor-wheeled tea-trolley will realize the problem straight away. In essence, the nose-wheel is not linked in any way to the brakes. The brakes operate the main wheels only. Thus, at slow speeds the only way to steer is with pressure left or right on the brakes, and the nosewheel must move accordingly. At higher speeds, the rudder comes into play and exerts its influence to give your directional stability.

Finally we arrived at the runway holding point – a series of yellow lines painted across the width of the taxiway.

'Brakes,' ordered Jock. 'You lock them on by pressing down on the pedals, pulling out that white knob to your left, hold, release brakes, release knob.'

I did as I was told.

'Throttle up to 1,000 revs. We shall check for a dead cut on the magnetos. Turn the ignition key two clicks to the left . . . now reset the key.'

I saw no appreciable loss of engine-power registering on the revs dial.

'Good. Wind her up to 1,700 revs to check for mag drop. Same procedure as before.'

Again I turned the key; again no substantial loss of power. In the event, I found out, as you will find out, that an aircraft has two independent magnetos – these supply all the electric power to the engine sparkplugs. It follows then that, in turning the key, you switch off each mag in turn and discover whether they are both serviceable.

'Let's see if the carburettor heat is functioning properly. Pull the black knob right out . . . hold it . . . now see what happens to the revs.' This time the needle fell back slightly.

'You can expect a ten per cent drop,' he said; and while it wasn't quite that much, it was close. 'Carburettor heat is necessary to prevent icing in the carb. You'll put it on for landings, and you'll check intermittently during flight if you suspect that ice may occur. A loss of engine power is the usual sign, but try not to let the situation develop that far.

'Just a few more vital actions to be performed now. Trim: slightly nose down for this aircraft. Mixture: rich. Tighten the nut at the base of the throttle lever. Pitch: it doesn't affect us; this is not a variable-pitch propeller. Fuel: on and sufficient. Flaps: as required. We shan't need any.'

I went through the motions, not fully realizing what was going on. In fact, what was going on happened to be my introduction to TMPFF – the initial letters of probably the most vital of vital actions. The mnemonic and its easily absorbed drill are given at the end of this chapter (p. 53). Take my tip and learn them now.

As I've explained, I wasn't particularly sure about any of this, but Jock seemed happy enough; and the way I saw it, if he was prepared to risk his neck, there couldn't be too much to worry about. He reached for the mike: 'Golf-uniform-foxtrot. Ready for take-off.'

Back came the reply: 'Golf-uniform-foxtrot. Hold position. Call tower one-one-eight-decimal-seven.'

Jock rotated the radio frequency dial to 118.7. 'Golf-uniform-foxtrot. Ready for take-off.'

'Roger, uniform-foxtrot. You are cleared via the ski-slope. Not above 2,000 feet VFR. Wind two-four-zero, twenty.'

Jock repeated back almost every word of the message.

What was he responding to? The ski-slope referred to is a well-known landmark for this particular airfield. Another is the bridges, meaning the Forth road and rail bridges. Thus they indicate a reference point for exit routes from the local control zone. Next, the 'not above 2,000 feet VFR' bit. When you earn your PPL, you will be duty-bound to stick to VFR – Visual Flight Rules. These state that before any flight you must have a visibility of five nautical miles. Additionally, once in the air, you and your aeroplane must be separated from cloud by 1,000 feet vertically, and horizontally by not less than one mile.

Incidentally, the rules change slightly if you continue your training and pick up an IMC rating (Instrument Meteorological Conditions), and drastically if you work for an Instrument Rating. For the purpose of this book, neither of these will come into consideration since we are after a PPL pure and simple.

So, they asked us to keep below 2,000 feet while in the control zone, because the larger fellows were entering at 3,000 feet or so and they wanted us where they could see us. Of course, once out of the zone, we could go to any height we wished – just so long as we stayed VFR.

'Roger, uniform-foxtrot,' agreed the tower, 'Line up and hold.'

Now I was told to open up and follow the taxiway onto runway two-six. There was no mistaking it; the 26 was painted on the threshold in huge white letters. Jock indicated to line up on the centre line and stop.

'When they give the word, throttle full on and hold the stick slightly back to take the weight off the nosewheel as she gains flying speed.' He then said something that brought me out in a cold sweat. 'Start pulling back at 60.' He pointed to the air-speed indicator. 'She'll come unstuck at 70.'

'How's that . . .?' I began, but was interrupted by the r/t.

'Uniform foxtrot. You are clear to take off. Wind two-four-zero, twenty. A left-hand turn into the circuit initially.'

By now, you will have enough knowledge to work out that two-four-zero was the wind direction i.e. blowing from 240°, and twenty its speed in knots.

UP, UP AND AWAY

Jock pointed along the runway. 'Away you go,' he said.

'You mean . . . ?'

'Away you go.'

'Oh, all right.' I pushed the throttle in hard – too hard. The engine roared, the plane leaped forward and the control column came out to meet me. I grabbed it, holding it rigid in a grip that had every knuckle white. The runway was rushing past fast – very fast, it seemed. I glued my eyes to the ASI . . . 30 . . . 40 . . . 50 . . . 60 . . . I started to pull back on the stick . . . nothing happened . . . 70 I eased the column towards me a little more . . . nothing . . . then a lot more . . . Suddenly, as though the aircraft had become a living breathing thing, I felt it respond. The nose came up, very slowly at first, then higher – much higher; and the engine developed a differently pitched note. We were airborne, up in the air, flying . . . and I was the one doing the flying!

I shot a glance to my right. Jock had his hands on his knees – nowhere near the control column. A copious dose of panic crept in – 'crashed in' might be a better expression. Perspiration started rolling and I couldn't understand why, because someone was holding ice-cubes against my spine. My heart was thumping like it was trying to get out; and I didn't blame it. Would I actually survive this experience? Did all his students do a take-off on their first lesson? If so, how many lasted the full course? What if he developed a heart attack? How the hell would we get back down? Would Lucky Lad win the 3.30 at Chepstow? Was I going to be alive to find out?

The ground was dropping away at a great rate, and there were bumps on the atmosphere.

'Keep the wings level,' Jock ordered. 'The model aircraft should be just on the centre line and straight.'

While all this was happening, I found myself making lots of adjustments to the stick – short, sharp, abrupt adjustments. Anyone on the ground should by then have been slapping their thighs and doubling up at our more than erratic progress. So far, I'd done nothing at all with the rudder pedals. In truth, my feet rested on them with a lightness most uncommon of my size nines – I was mortified at the idea of using the rudder in case some irreversible event occurred.

Jock lifted a hand from his knee and indicated to turn left. 'That's left stick and left rudder,' he said. 'Easy, easy . . . now take off some of the bank by holding the stick against the turn.'

It was rather like using opposite lock when a car runs into a skid – and, brother, were we skidding. Not enough rudder was the reason, but I didn't find out about that until my second lesson.

After what seemed forever, Jock said: 'All right, I have control. I've got her.'

'Can we smoke?' I asked, reaching with shaking hands for fags and lighter and barely able to open the pack.

'Most certainly. Let's both have one.'

In retrospect, the rest of the flight was pretty uneventful. At the time, however, the experience was nothing less than traumatic. I took control intermittently, and every time I did so it became very apparent, since the aeroplane suddenly realized the fact and then flew anywhere it fancied. You will probably discover that your first aeroplane does exactly the same: it will fly crab-wise; it will fly one wing down; and it will suddenly climb for no apparent reason. And all of this in spite of your very best efforts.

For fun, Jock navigated us twenty miles into the Borders and we flew right over my house. And that really was a surprise. The garden that I had always thought was something on hire to the jungle warfare establishment looked amazingly tidy from the air. I made up my mind that, if ever we decided to sell, I would show prospective buyers over the place from 1,000 feet.

Landing was delightful, of course. I've never been so glad to be somewhere in my entire life. But, oddly, as we were taxi-ing back to the club, someone – and I swear it wasn't me – said: 'D'you really think you could teach a dumb-bell like me to fly?'

'Of course.'

'D'you think I should bother?'

'In what way?'

'Well, will I be any good?'

'I don't see why not.' But the way he said it, I got the distinct impression that he didn't see *why* either. Or, indeed, how.

'What about cash?'

'The complete course will cost around £2,000. That includes fifteen hours in the classroom.'

As it turned out, I paid quite a bit less, but I was fortunate in having an instructor who insisted on giving full value for every penny and who therefore would not clock up extra hours simply for the revenue. Thus, at 1983 rates, I got a real bargain. One more very good reason for choosing your club with care.

'And do people normally pay up-front?' I asked.

'Not as a rule – just pay as you go.'

'All right,' I said. 'Let's do it.'

And we did.

SUMMARY

Vital Action Pre Take-Off

TMPFF

T. Trim for take-off. Tighten throttle nut.
M. Mixture rich. Carburettor heat – check.
P. Pitch fine.
F. Fuel on and sufficient. Fuel pressure. Oil pressure. Oil temperature.
F. Flaps – as required. All instruments stable. Harness and hatches secure.

Get to know your Aircraft

If you can, always arrive early for your flying lessons. This allows briefing time for the instructor and also gives you the opportunity to sit inside the aircraft on the ground and familiarize yourself with the instruments and the controls. Examine each of them minutely and get to know their locations on the panel intimately. A few minutes spent like this will pay dividends once you're in the air. There's nothing worse than being ordered by your instructor to 'watch that airspeed' when you cannot for the life of you locate the airspeed indicator.

Learn the Pre-Take-off Drill by Heart

Apart from TMPFF, you will also need to know how to conduct an examination of the exterior of your aircraft before take-off. Fortunately, manufacturers provide specially printed handbooks which detail pre-flight, in-flight and shut-down procedures. Your club should have a good supply of these, and if you can't pinch one, photostat one and learn by rote everything it contains.

Getting to Grips with ATC

Should you experience initial difficulty understanding Air Traffic Control r/t procedure, there are a number of firms which specialize in r/t courses via cassette tapes. A further way to improve your intimacy with the people in the tower is to ask them to allow you to sit with them and monitor their broadcasts. Either way, you will quickly catch on to the jargon. But never be afraid to ask for a message to be repeated, several times *and slowly* if necessary; and never pretend that you have understood a message when you haven't. That road leads to disaster.

QNH and QFE

These are the codes for barometric pressures. Their values are given in millibars. (One millibar equals thirty feet at sea-level.) As I've said in the text, QNH represents the pressure at mean sea-level while QFE applies to pressure at airfield level. A simple way to remember which is which is, QNH: Q Not Home and QFE: Q Field Elevation.

4. The Exploratory Hours

The build-up to the big event – that first solo flight – is several hours of increasingly adept handling, punctuated by seconds of sheer terror when you over-reach yourself.

First, you must get to know the aircraft. Just as with a new car or a new pair of shoes even, you have to feel it out and wear it in.

Second, you must get to know yourself. That may sound a little psycho-puerile, but you could well be surprised how your demeanour, even your basic character, will alter once behind a control column. And I'm not simply talking about these sudden changes of attitude that overcome most humans when in sudden fear of their lives – which often result in the lifelong atheist suddenly breaking into sixteen bars of 'Abide with Me'. I don't mean that at all. The changes I refer to are usually quite subtle ones: the very cocky types lose a little of their strut, while the quiet and reserved ones begin to talk – albeit nervous chatter – more than hitherto.

I witnessed these personality transmutations over a period of months in the students who began flying at around the same time as I. I was also aware of it happening to me. In the clubhouse bar after a day's flying, blokes who would never have admitted to making a mistake in their lives rapidly and unselfconsciously blurted out their errors of the day.

That's what the formative flying hours do to you, and for you, and I believe it's all to the good.

GETTING THE FEEL OF THINGS

Those early hours are extremely important. Depending on how quickly you catch on – and, more significantly, how consistently you perform – your instructor will work hard to advance your first solo flight to the earliest possible moment, and allow you that once-in-a-lifetime privilege.

How many hours before you go solo? Rumour has it that the average is ten. Some people do it in six, others take sixteen. Frankly, I took nine full hours, although even then I didn't believe I was ready. So the answer to the question is this: you'll know deep within yourself when it's time to cut the umbilical cord.

I made a personal log of all hours flown. Here are the three hours, following the initial flight, in brief, to give you an idea of what's in store.

HOUR TWO
Cockpit briefing – cursory.
Self take-off.
Fear. Wet palms.
Level flight – artificial horizon.
Tentative, panic-ridden turns.
Can't understand ATC r/t.

HOUR THREE
Cockpit briefing – less cursory.
Self take-off.
Fear.
Steeper turns – too much drift.
Stall principles! Moderate. Engine throttled back. Stall warning buzzer. No *real* stall.
Landing explained.
Still can't understand ATC.

HOUR FOUR
Tough cockpit briefing.
Self take-off.
Less fear.
Better turns – non-skid.
Serious stall exercises.
Landing – did it together. Terror!
Have given up trying to understand ATC!!

From this you will understand just how pathetic a student I was. The flying was dreadfully important, of course, but so was self-preservation. In the early days, stalling exercises held a very real terror – now they're just like stepping off a log.

But why, you might ask, would anybody in their right mind deliberately and wittingly stall an aircraft? The principle of this, and of all the other exercises you will need to perform, is simply (a) to give you handling confidence, (b) to recognize a particular problem, such as a stall, when you're in one, so that you may efficiently and safely fly your way out of it.

I'll agree that you have to be some kind of a lulu to stall a modern single-engined trainer accidentally. Yet it can be done – and fatally done – which is reasonable motivation for knowing what to do about it when it happens.

The same applies to spinning. Only a masochist would purposely put a plane into an aggravated spin. I dislike it intensely. And it's a real work of art to spin any of today's training planes. But, again, some aircraft will spin of their own volition if improperly handled. So it's a good idea to be able to apply the appropriate correction and live to tell the tale.

Incidentally, the CAA no longer requires the student to undertake spinning exercises as mandatory for the PPL licence – largely, I suppose, for the reasons given above, in that the probability factor in most modern ships is less than nil. If your instructor, however, is anything like my instructor, he will demand that you at least know what the experience feels like and can recognize it if it ever happens again. Always remember: if you do get into a spin and are about to make your encroachment on eternity, the CAA won't be sitting beside you!

EFFECTS OF THE CONTROLS

What we should be talking about are the various flight exercises and how they're accomplished. Indeed, let's discuss the control surfaces and how they operate at the same time.

First, the ailerons; they give you control in the *rolling plane*.

Turn the control column left, and the plane will bank left-wing down, i.e. it will turn left. It does this because the left aileron rises, forcing that wing down, while the right

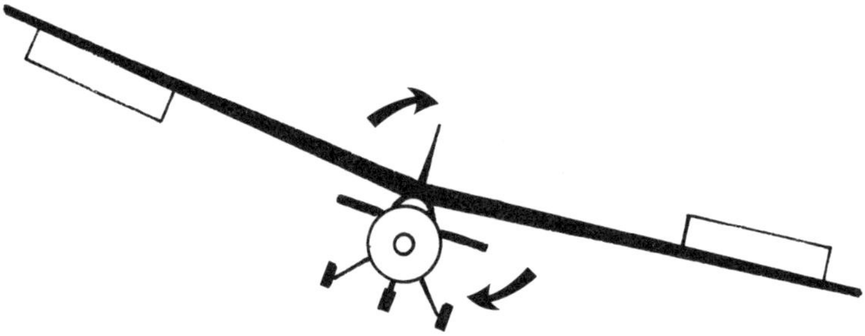

Fig. 6. Stick to the left = port aileron up, starboard aileron down. The result is a roll to the left. Therefore the opposite applies when the stick is moved right

aileron drops, lifting that wing up. Were you to leave that bank uncorrected – by keeping the column hard left – the aircraft would descend and perform the proverbial ever-decreasing circles ritual until finally, with a flash, a bang, a shower of green feathers . . . you know the rest.

Thus bank must be corrected. This is done by moving the column very gently against the accumulating rate of bank. In other words, in a left turn you move the wheel left, then ease on a touch of right-hand wheel. This axiom applies whether you are turning right to left or whether you're performing a shallow turn or a steep one.

To prevent yourself skidding all over the sky, and to make your turns real turns rather than back-end drifts, you bring the rudder into play. The rudder gives you control in the *yawing plane*; so when you push on the left-hand rudder pedal, the nose of the aircraft will move left, and conversely for the right-hand pedal.

Now, when you use the rudder in conjunction with the control column, side-slip is virtually eliminated and skid is brought under control. Therefore, to make a half-descent left turn, it's left stick and left rudder in unison, not forgetting that minor stick adjustment mentioned above to prevent a spiral dive developing. Moreover, you will discover as you go along that a slight backward pressure on the stick in a left-hand turn, and a slight forward pressure in a right-hand turn, will keep the nose of the machine tracing the horizon beautifully.

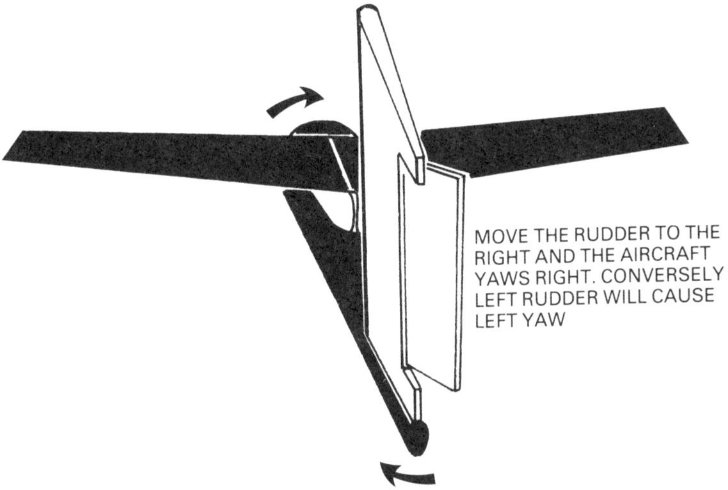

Fig. 7. Rudder and yaw demonstration

You can, of course, use rudder only to correct yaw in certain circumstances – on a landing approach, for instance. But just as with the ailerons, if you leave rudder on, a roll will eventually develop in that direction.

Elevators, next. They control the aircraft in the *pitching plane* – i.e. tail down, nose up. Pull back on the stick and the nose will rise, your angle of attack relative to the airflow will increase, and your speed will drop. Too much back pressure combined with too little speed results in a stall. From this it can be seen that the elevator not only helps you to climb and descend: it also helps control your forward speed. You will use it with impunity on approaches to land.

We'd better include flaps here, and find out exactly what their function is. To sum it up in a few words: an aircraft has flaps to increase lift and drag, while lowering the stalling speed.

Let's analyse that. The lowering of flap increases a wings lift. It also creates drag. Yet lift and drag are not increased in equal proportions – the more flap we apply, the less beneficial is our lift and the more aggravated our drag. All of which shows there's an optimum degree of flap for the maximum amount of lift. On the matter of flap having the effect of lowering stalling speed, it simply means you can fly that much slower with flaps down than you'd normally be able to without stalling.

We can now see why we apply flap when about to land. It gives us the ability to fly at the lowest possible speed for a safe touchdown.

Our last control surface is the trim tab. You'll locate it at the trailing edge of, and working independently from, the elevator – that's the starboard elevator on Cessna 150s. You operate it via a notched wheel set beneath the instrument panel.

What happens is this. The airflow over the trim tab holds the elevators in any desired position simply by adjustment of the wheel. This means, in effect, that if you set the tab for straight and level flight, you need exert no pressure on the stick to hold it straight in the *pitching plane*. The same applies if you set it for a climb or a glide. It's a sort of auto-pilot, but it isn't – since you wouldn't trust it for any length of time farther than you could chuck it. It does, however, relieve you of a lot of the work; and it's just the job when you need to fly hands-off while you check a map or light a fag. The trim tab, of course, does not help you control the aircraft in the *rolling plane*, although in fair weather without turbulence or too much wind the aircraft will remain stable for quite long periods hands-off.

Clearly, the more you know about airframes and engines at the start of your flying training the better. But the foregoing, if you absorb it and remember it, is about all you need in the early hours.

On the subject of learning and remembering, I found the whole process extremely difficult. What with being well over forty, which didn't help, and having long ago lost the art of storing things away, I was plagued by another problem. In my occupation as freelance advertising copywriter, I take briefings from clients as diverse in their character as, for instance, the technology of body-scanners, the comparative rpms of domestic spin-dryers, and the social and economical advantages of investing in a certain car, or particular branded beverage. Who would want to retain that little lot for any length of time? So over the years I've trained myself to remember the facts of the matter for just as long as it takes to get them down on paper – then I've deliberately expunged them. This has now become a cerebral habit, one totally antipathetic to the learning process – a circumstance with which my flying instructor would no doubt readily concur. My brain is like Teflon – nothing sticks.

It only confirms an earlier statement: if I can do it, anybody can do it.

BASIC MANŒUVRES

Let's assume you want to discover more about the basic flight manœuvres you'll have to learn. They are: straight and level flight, climbing, descending, turning, stalling, stall turns, spinning, take-off, circuits, approach and landing.

Some we've already discussed, and later we'll talk about circuit work and landing. Right now, let's take you through a spinning exercise. Are you strapped in?

Before you undertake a spin, or indeed any boisterous manœuvre, there are certain procedures to adopt. You can remember them with the aid of the initials HASELL. This word represents the vital actions to be undertaken on *all* spinning and stalling exercises.

H = Height: For a spin it's a recovery height of 3,000 feet.

A = Airframe: Flaps up, trim neutral, instruments balanced.

S = Security: harness and hatches secure, no loose articles in the cockpit.

E = Engine: check carburettor heat, mags operating, suction, fuel on and sufficient.

L = Location: not over a built-up area.

L = Look out: perform a 360° inspection turn

Now you're ready to spin, so here's the principle. Approach the stall as previously indicated, with the nose well above the horizon, and just before the aircraft actually stalls, slap on hard left rudder and pull the stick completely back. Unless you've cheated, the aircraft should now be spinning – working its way towards the ground, yawing, pitching and rolling. Apart from throwing up all over the carpet, you'd better make some contribution to the situation, thus to get back onto an even keel.

Here's what you do. Full right rudder – that's the opposite direction to the spin entry; then stick forward gently. This action will probably cause the plane to spin faster, but no problem, that's a good sign. Eventually the spin will cease, and at that immediate stage centralize the rudder and pull back on the stick. The nose will rise slowly and you can apply power as soon as the horizon comes up nice and straight ahead of you.

Not so bad was it? Well, chum, you can do all my spins in future. I loathe them with an intensity that would make lightbulbs glow. I need spinning like a moose needs a hat-rack! But you, well, you'll probably love every minute of it!

At some time or another, you'll have to undertake some low-level flying. That means flying at heights well below the statutory limits.

An aircraft other than a helicopter, says the book, shall not fly below 1,500 feet *above* the highest fixed object which is within 2,000 feet of it horizontally. Also, you can't fly within 1,000 yards of any assembly in the open that consists of more than 1,000 people unless you have written permission from the CAA. That'll stop you giving impromptu air displays, won't it? Finally, no aeroplane may fly nearer than 500 feet to any person, building or vehicle. The latter, of course, is null and void when you're landing and taking off.

My low-flying exercises were something to remember – as yours will no doubt be.

It happened completely out of the blue. We were returning from outside the control zone, where Jock had been instructing me on tight turns when ATC told us to hold off because they were expecting Purple traffic. 'Purple' is the official appellation given to aircraft carrying members of the Royal Family, which, of course, have priority over everything else. In any event, we meandered around for a while, to find ourselves over the Firth of Forth some twelve miles from Edinburgh.

'After all that hard work on turns, I'm going to give you a treat,' said Jock. 'Let's tell 'em what we're doing.' He reached for the mike. 'Edinburgh tower, this is golf-uniform-foxtrot. My position is three miles south of Kirkcaldy. Height: 2,000 feet. Request clearance for low-flying detail west towards the bridges.'

Back came ATC: 'Roger, golf-uniform-foxtrot. Draw your attention to obstruction at Burntisland.'

The benefit of flying low over water is there's nothing much to run into, you're infringing no air laws, and you don't make a nuisance of yourself to those people on the ground taking a nap or sunbathing in the plum.

Jock did his usual hand-signal. 'Right, take her down,' he said. 'Level out at 100 feet and keep her that way.' There was a pause. 'If you can.'

I put the plane into a steep descending bank, levelling off at the required height. We were over water some 500 yards from land.

Jock made a cautionary gesture. 'Follow the shoreline, but keep this exact distance from it. Away you go.'

And away I went, belting down the Forth, often lower than the buildings on the shore. It was a superb feeling knowing that people sitting in their living-rooms had to lean forward and look down to see the lunatic flier hedge-hopping the ships below.

The experience was another in the long list of buzzes one gets learning to fly. Buildings, shore projections, lighthouses and small boats came and went at an amazing rate, even though our speed was no more than ninety. The water seemed touchable, and in those moments when I took my eyes off the altimeter and the artificial horizon to watch a landmark go by, we'd drop to about eighty feet – which I'd hastily correct with a bashful grin and a thumping heart.

It was a great detail, and a lesson well learned. If ever I'm caught out by lowering cloud miles from an airfield, I'll be confident enough to get close to the deck and virtually drive home.

The obstruction at Burntisland which ATC had warned us about was, in fact, a 1,040-foot television transmitter. I saw it coming, took avoiding action and missed it by a good half-mile.

TAKE-OFF AND LANDING

We've covered a good deal of ground, thus far; what we haven't said much about is take-off and landing. I'll put that right.

Take-off, in my humble opinion, on a decent runway with the moving parts and works at optimum performance, is no big problem. It's about as easy as dating a lady in a Shanghai cathouse with a sack of rice on your back.

Landing, on the other hand, can be compared with trying to attempt the above with a sack of rattlesnakes. It ain't easy. What's more, it takes a lot of practice before it becomes any the easier.

Let's say no more about take-off, then, except to give the obvious advice that you always take off into the wind, with full power, and with the nose at an attitude which will accommodate that power without stalling – i.e. at not too great an angle of attack. A take-off in a crosswind, when it's blowing across your bows, is a touch more difficult. In that event, you simply hold the plane on the runway for a little longer than usual, then steer nose into the wind as you leave the tarmac to counter any drift.

Approach and landing, as I've said, are a different game altogether, and we must delve into them quite thoroughly.

One way or another, every flight you make will always result in a landing – and I emphasize the 'one way or another'. So getting it right every time is more or less mandatory. Furthermore, and very seriously, you won't be able to solo until you're reasonably consistent with touchdowns.

To enlarge upon that, it's a well broadcast fact that my own early landings were nothing short of dreadful. They were arrivals rather than well-thought-out, carefully calculated put-downs. I did more overshoots than a grouse moor on 12 August; my abort-and-go-round-agains were becoming a standard joke in the club bar. Not only that: on the occasions when I did manage to make contact with the concrete, the impression I gave was more that of a precipitation of angle-iron from a great height. Wallop! And the resultant shock wave must have put windows out for miles around.

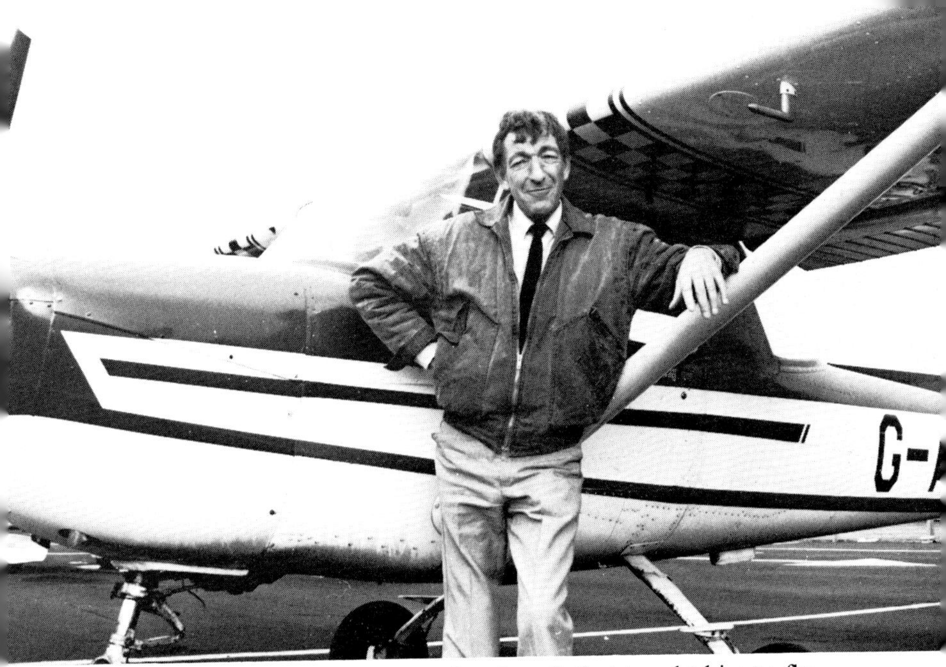

The author with Uniform-Fox – the aircraft that taught him to fly. She may not be as fast or as pretty as some – but she has a lot of character

Often described as 'the Ford of the air', the basic design of the Cessna 150 makes it a very forgiving aircraft. And G-AXUF has exonerated an entire generation of student pilots

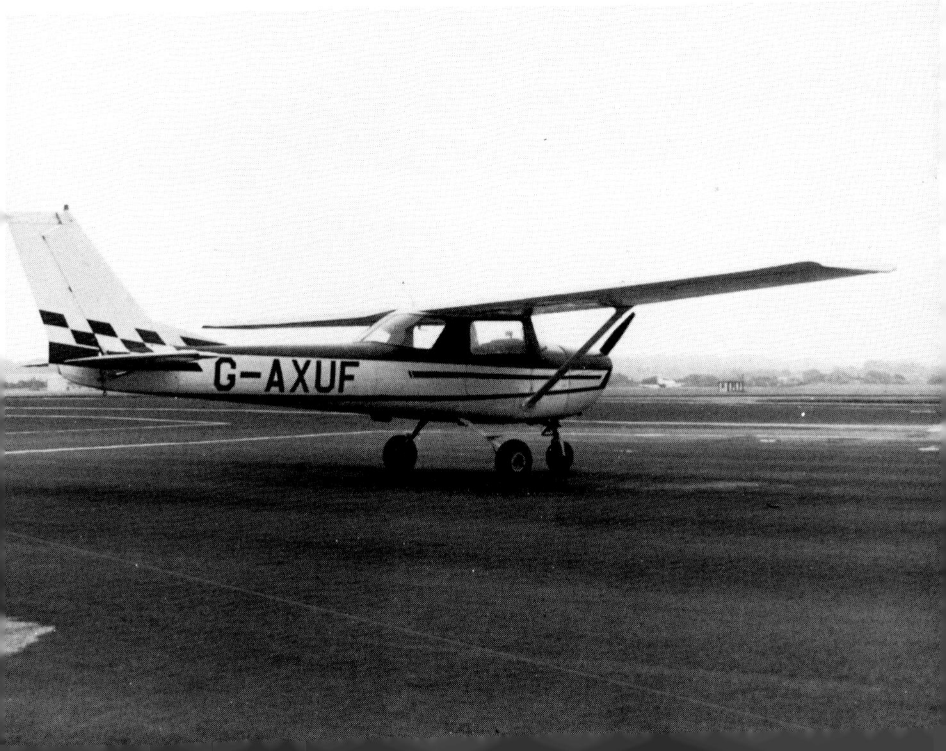

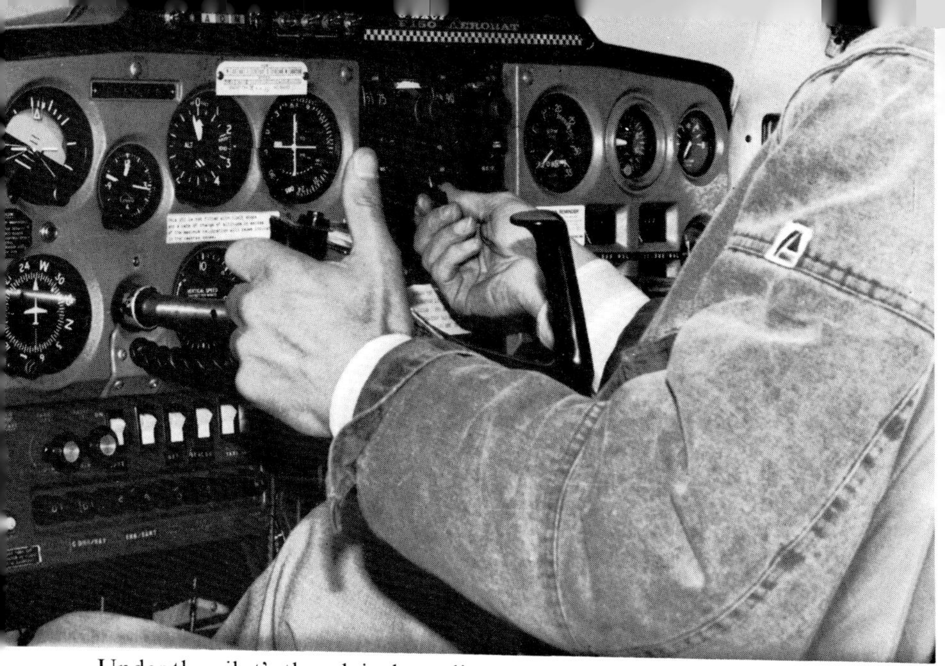

Under the pilot's thumb is the radio 'transmit' button. But according to the altimeter – third dial from the left – he is flying underground!

Jock Dalgleish explaining the intricacies of a 150's landing gear. 'It doesn't retract – unless of course you come down too hard!'

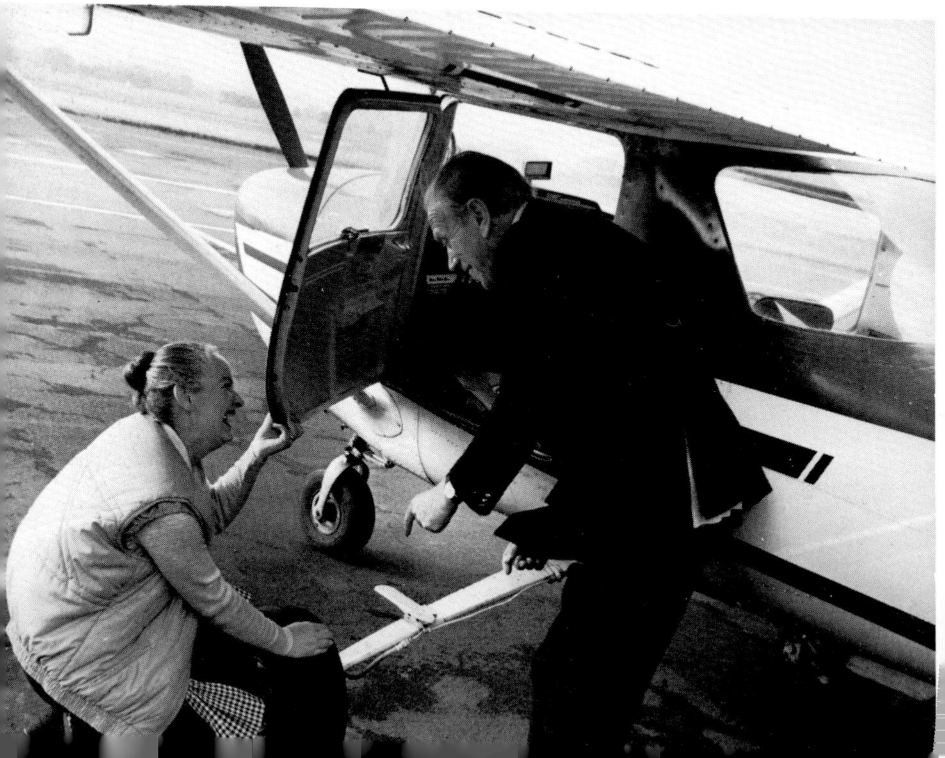

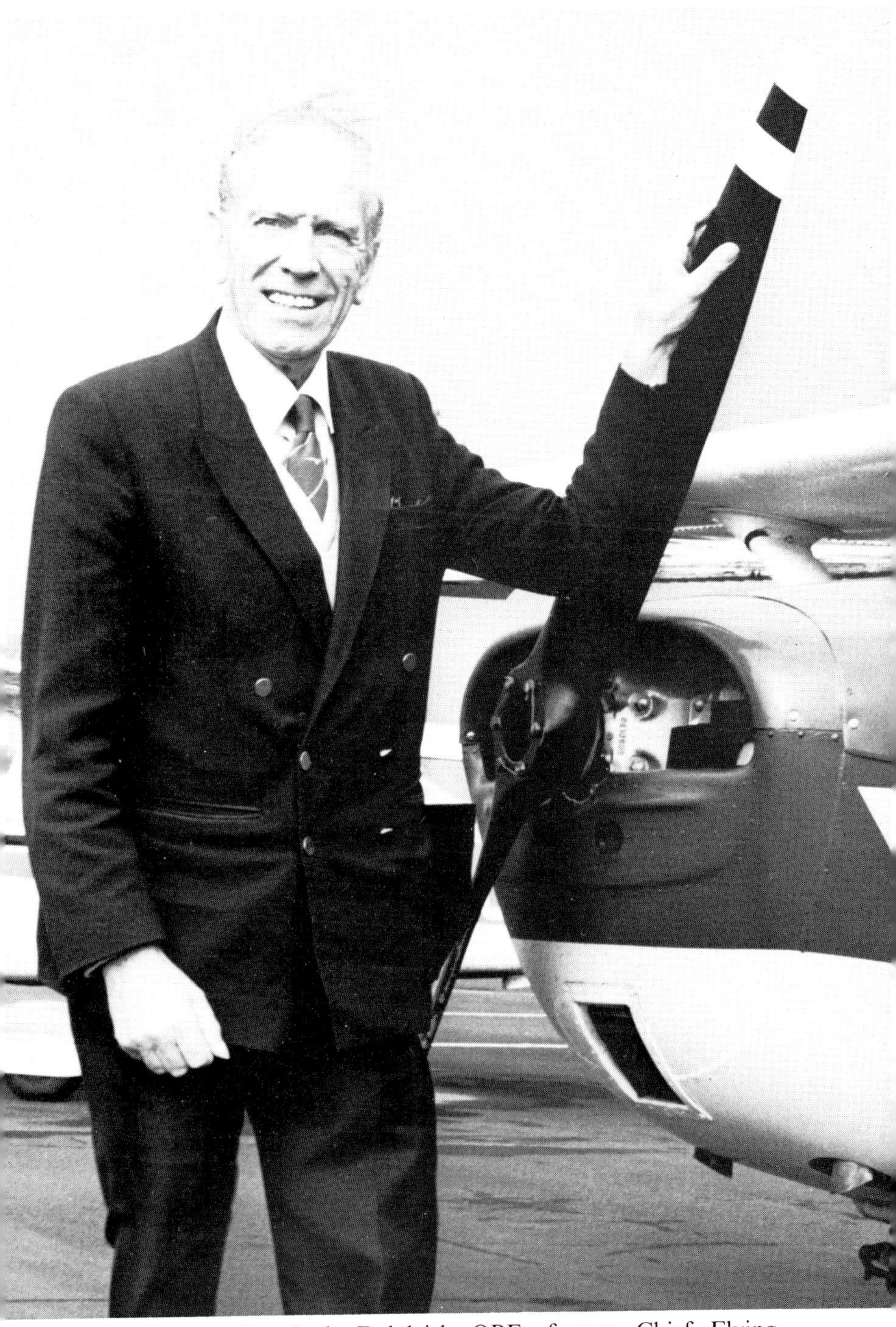

Wing-Commander Jock Dalgleish OBE, former Chief Flying Instructor of Turnhouse Flying Club and the author's guru

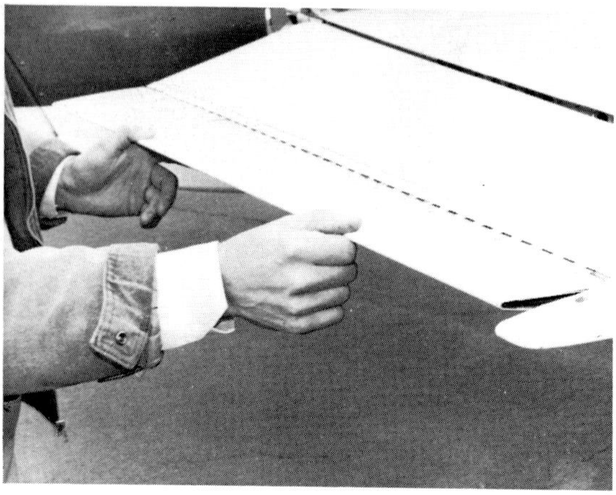

The trim tab (see Chapter 3). Properly used, this control surface takes the 'weight' off the elevators and takes the effort out of maintaining the aircraft's pitch attitude

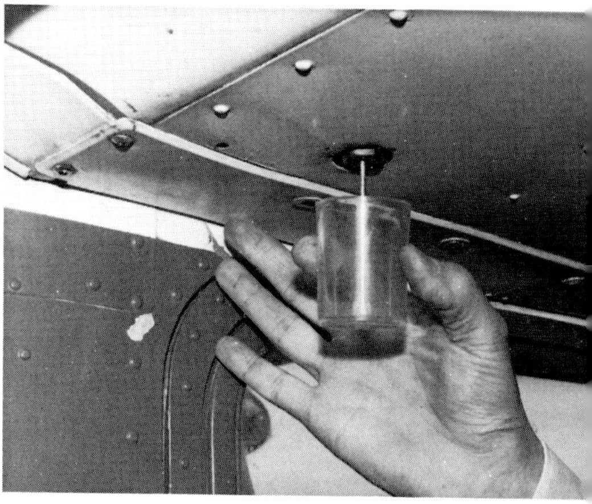

Checking a wing-mounted fuel tank for water deposits. Water in the fuel lines can cause serious engine trouble; but its presence is easily detected using this method

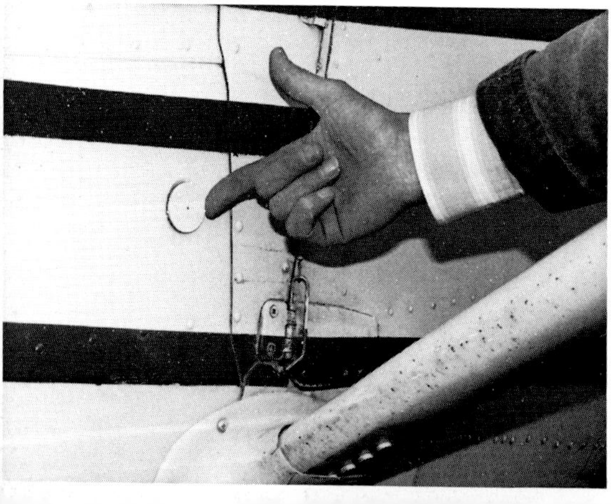

The static vent located on the forward fuselage. The pin-hole in the centre takes 'samples' of air to operate the altimeter and the vertical speed indicator. It also works in conjuction with the pitot tube for operation of the airspeed indicator.

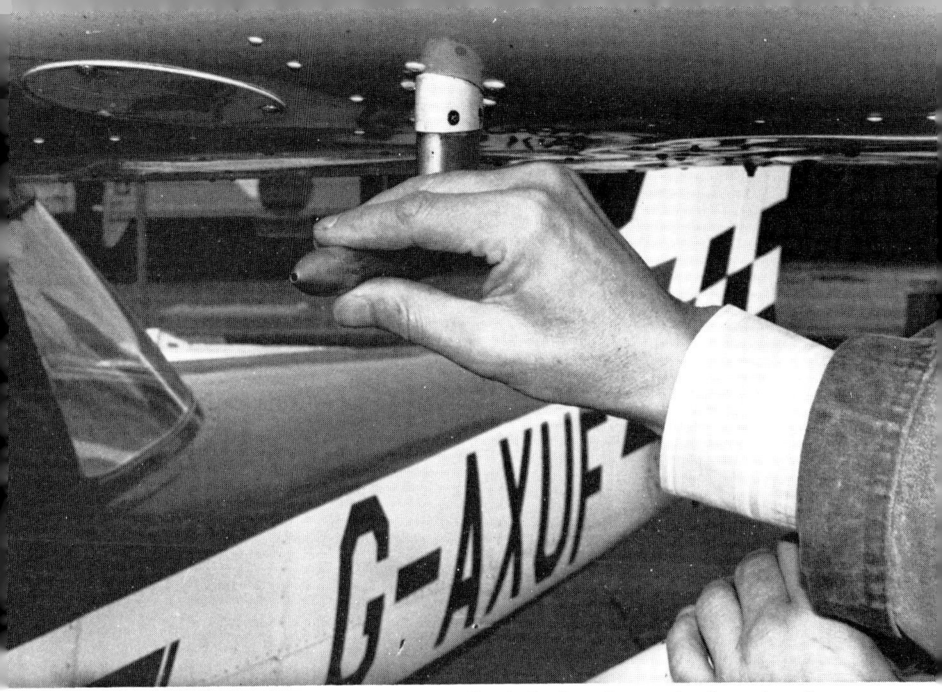

The pitot tube. Another 'air-sampling' device, its main function is to operate the airspeed indicator. This Cessna 150 pitot tube is slung beneath the wing facing the airflow. It thus receives the full force of the air pressure

Inspecting flap linkages prior to a flight. A good pilot examines the aircraft end to end before every trip – even though it may have been flown only minutes beforehand

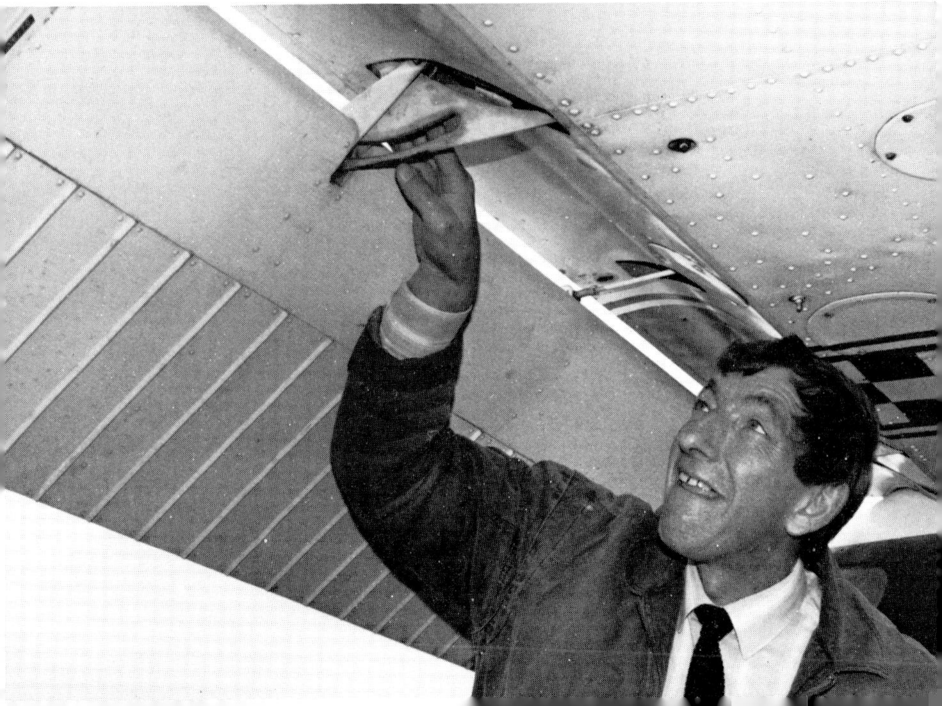

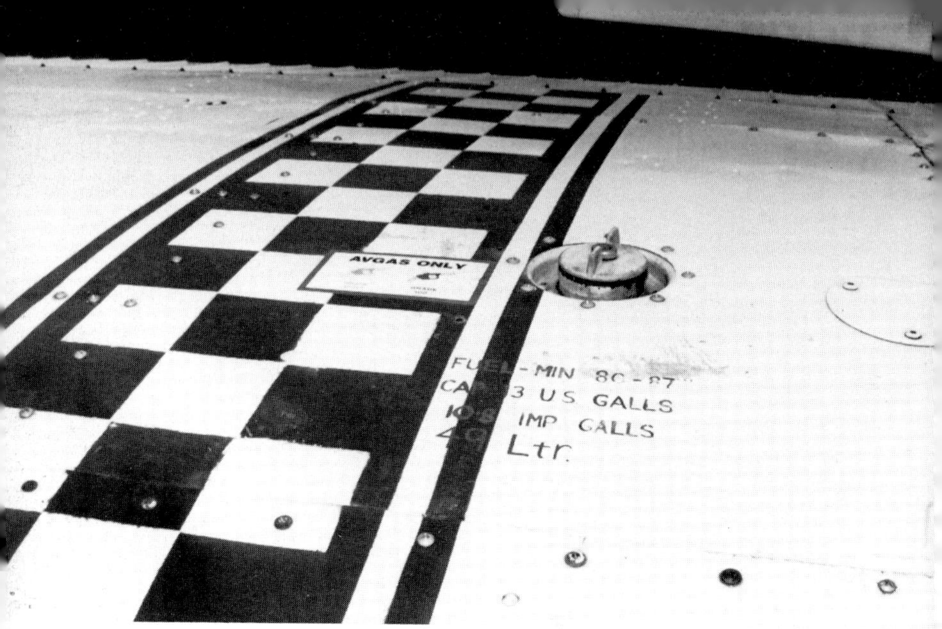

A close-up of a wing-tank fuel filler-cap. Note the warning that the aircraft burns aviation fuel (Avgas) only. This helps prevent the use of unsuitable motor fuel (Mogas) – particularly when operating from 'away' airfields where bowser operators are not familiar with you or your aircraft

The hydraulic brake system must be inspected for fluid leakage before every trip. No brakes can come as quite a shock on a short strip airfield. Additionally, the almost treadless tyre is designed to give minimum ground-drag at take-off and maximum grip on the touch-down roll-out

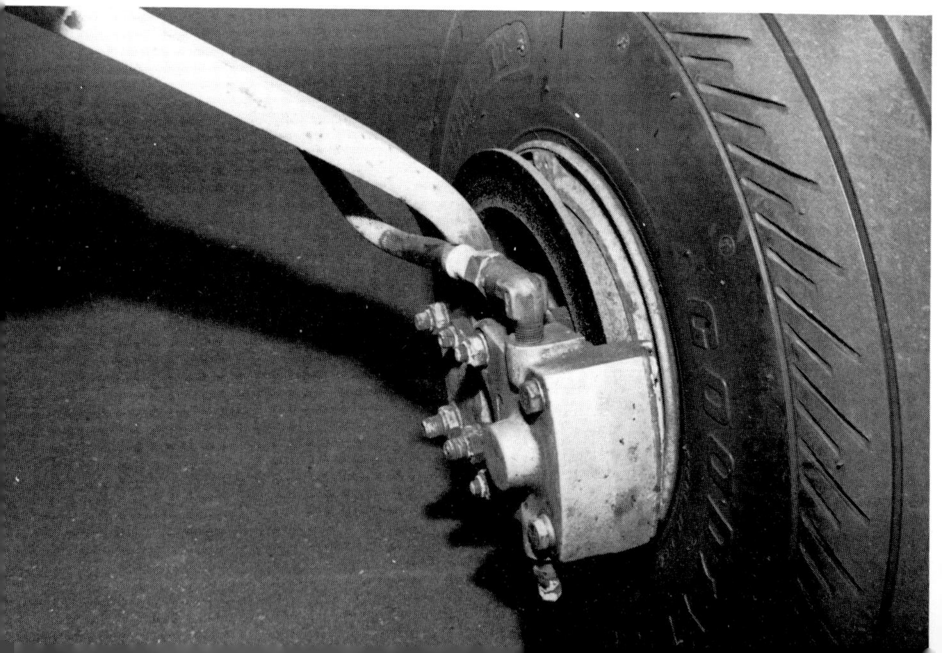

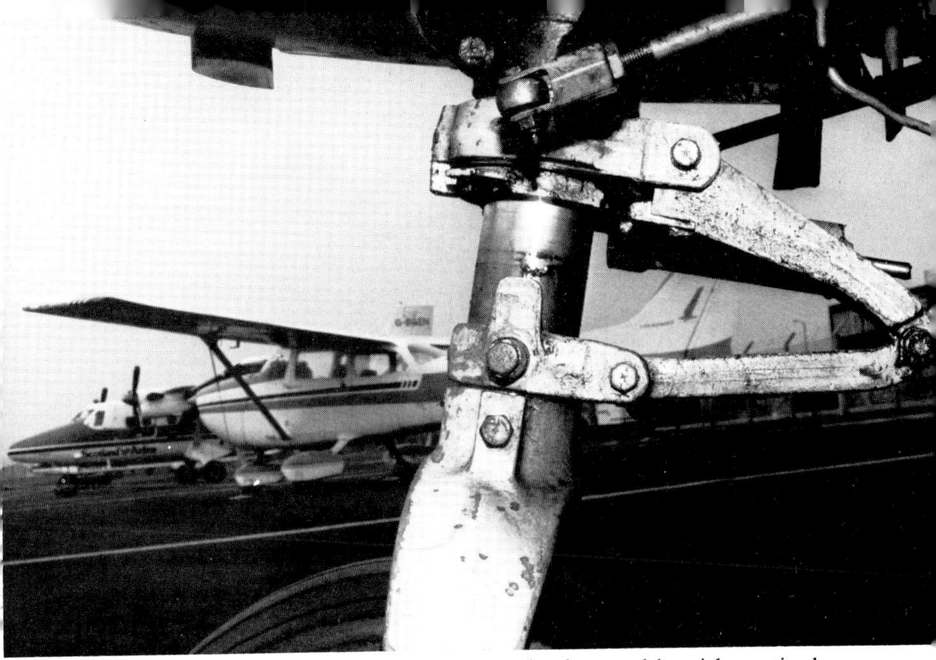

A ground-level shot of the 150's nose-wheel assembly with particular reference to the oleo – the damper-rod which 'floats' between the upper and lower brackets. Operationally, the oleo should show exactly 3″ of visible rod

The flight-deck of the Cessna 150: G-AXUF. A simple and easy-to-scan instrument panel makes this aircraft an ideal trainer

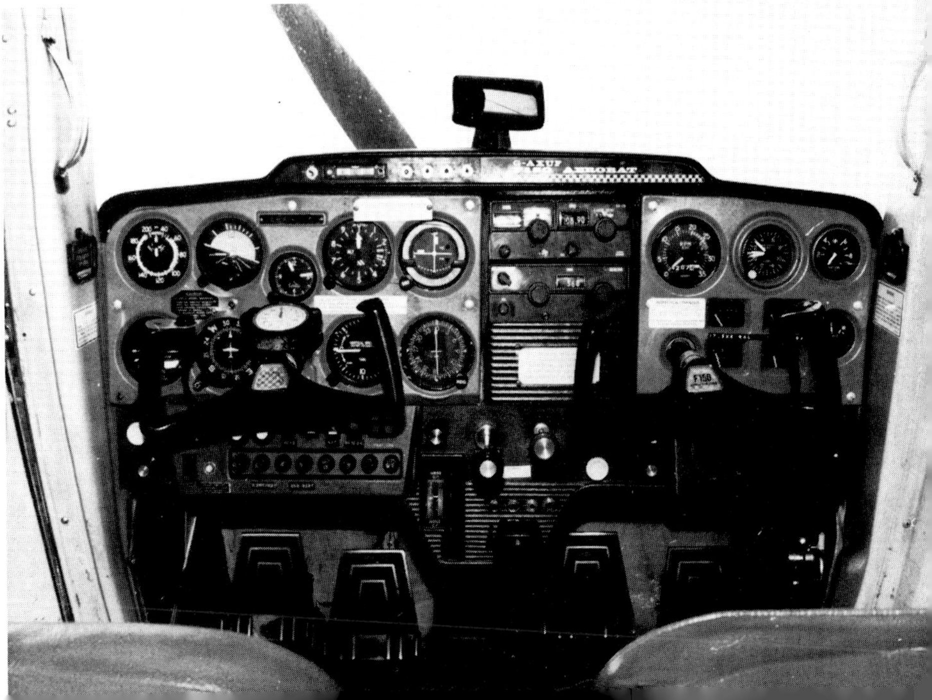

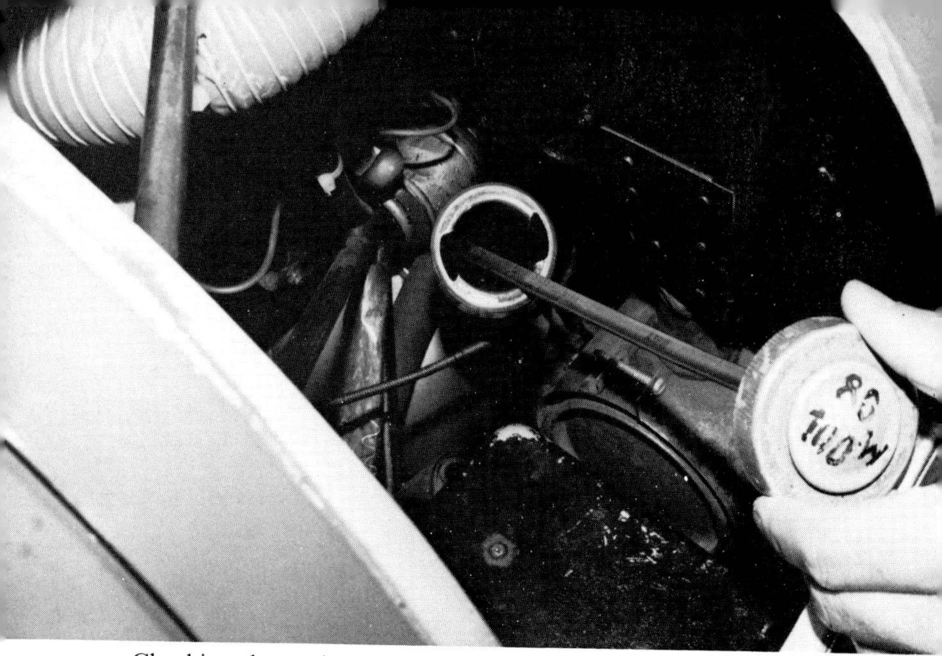

Checking the engine-oil level by means of a dip-stick located inside the nose cowling. It's exactly the same procedure as for a motor car, but with possibly more serious consequences should it be neglected

Jock Dalgleish and a student pilot either inspecting Uniform-Fox's propeller or figuring out how to wind up the elastic!

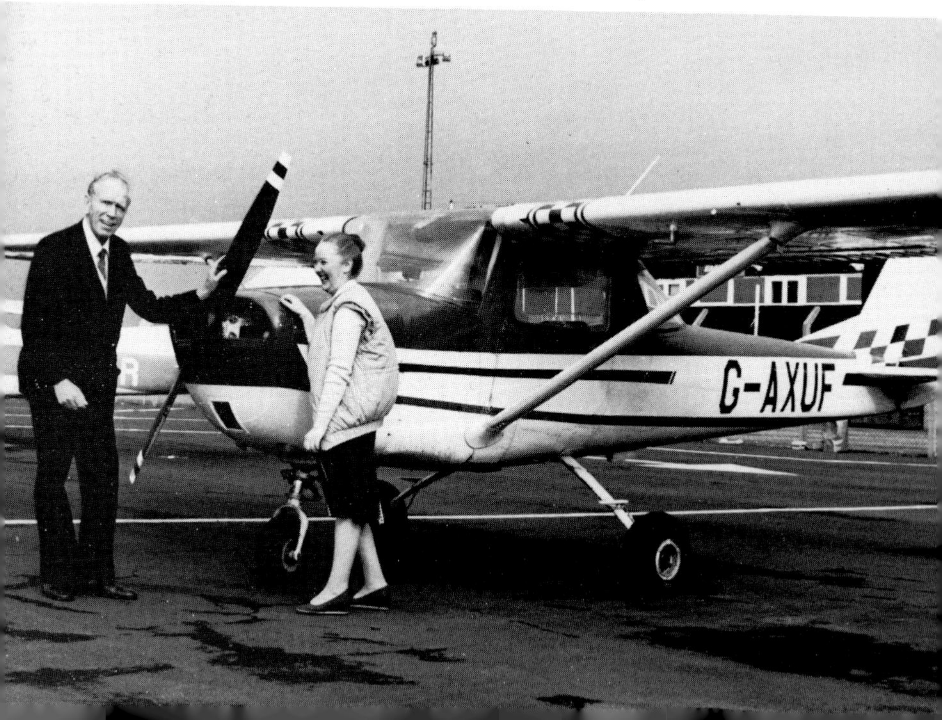

So had I applied myself, perhaps I could have solo-ed a lot sooner.

Which only goes to show how very tolerant and persevering flying instructors can be. Mine barely turned a hair; not outwardly anyway. Even after one excruciatingly bad touch-down, all he said, was: 'I wasn't quite looking for that, you know.'

So instead of going off his trolley, as he was well entitled to do, he counselled me with an avuncular concern – the gist of which I pass on to you. I'll do so in reverse order, as the saying goes, working backwards from the touchdown, because to my illogical mind it's the logical way.

First, when you attempt to put down a plane that's equipped with a tricycle undercarriage, the main wheels must touch first. You hold off by pulling *back* on the stick before lowering the nosewheel gently onto the runway. Were you to make the unforgivable mistake of going in nosewheel first, you'd be the unhappy driver of an erratic and uncontrollable wheel-barrow.

Second, in getting those main wheels to touch, you need to adopt a less than steep but more than shallow angle of approach. This entails getting the aeroplane nicely set up on the way in, so that at the appropriate moment it can be gradually *rounded out* to check the downward trend.

Rounding out means, simply, that you pull back to bring the plane parallel with the ground. Obviously, the closer you are to the deck when this happens – though not too close – the better, because, given that you have throttled right back, increased the drag with a touch of flap, the aircraft will lose headway and begin to sink. Which is exactly what you're looking for. To counteract excessive sink, the pilot gradually puts more back pressure on the control column and, with any luck, if he's close enough to the tarmac, he'll lay the under-carriage down like gossamer threads on a rose bloom. That last part of the process is called the *hold-off*. See Fig. 8.

At what height during the approach do you begin to round out, and how can you tell when? Don't ask me; and were you to put the question to more experienced pilots, you'd

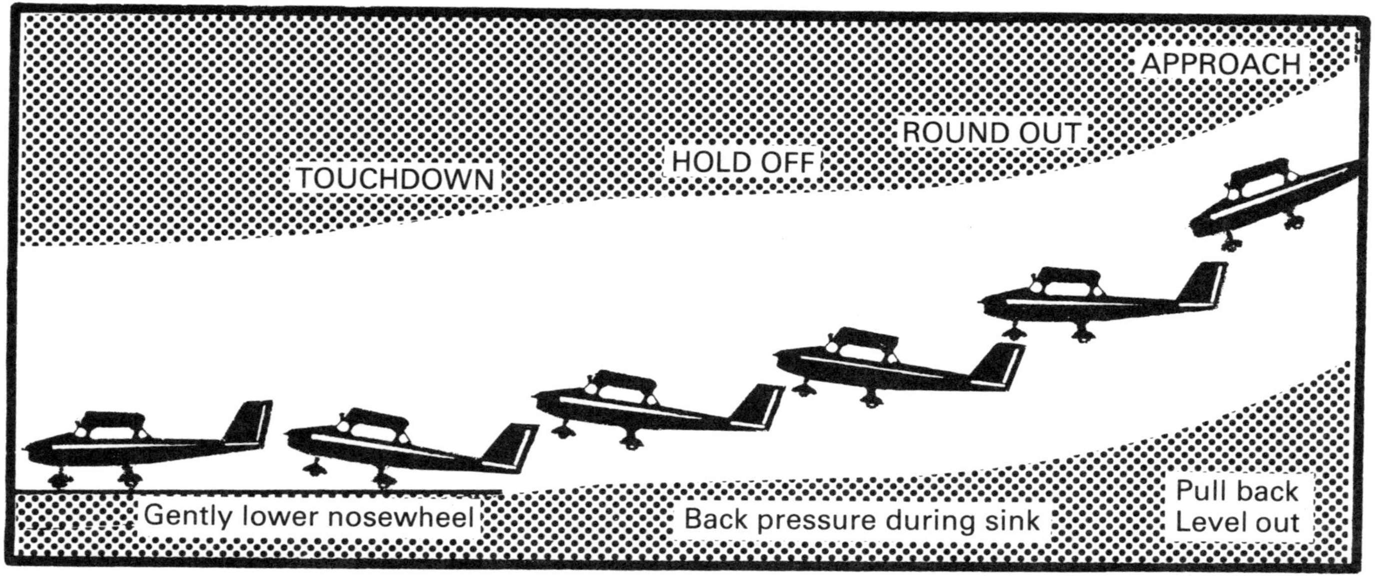

Fig. 8. Landing sequence. Judging the height of the round out is an acquired art that takes much practice. Note that during the sink we gradually apply more and more back pressure on the stick . . . pressure rather than pull

only receive the same answer. You have to do it to know it.

Personally, I've evolved a method whereby impromptu alarm gongs start sounding in my head, and I know I must start levelling the nose-down attitude. Another, more scientific way is that aspects of the runway and surrounding areas take on a certain configuration in the windscreen as you descend, so when the pattern is just right, you do what you have to do. Not that I round out at the identical height every time – far from it. Indeed, it's arguable whether I've ever done it twice the same way. What usually happens is, depending on my approach speed, any crosswind, the FT index and whether the bank manager realizes we're overdrawn yet, the plane somehow levels itself some half-a-dozen feet above the runway.

The remainder of the touchdown should be no accident. Patience is the keyword; the ability to sit there composedly, slowly losing height, rapidly eating runway and gently easing back on the stick to increase the angle of attack in an effort to slow the aircraft down to a tarmac-acceptable speed, finally to grease the wheels down like oil pouring on glass. That bit is an art which comes only with perseverance. I can say, in honesty, that I've done it thus only the once. Doubtless an accident.

My experience is that, if you try to rush things, you always cock it up. Rushing, for instance, will cause a bounce. That's where you hit and rebound quite unnervingly. Rushing will also cause ballooning. Here you pull back too quickly and too hard on the round-out, and the plane floats skyward with very little forward momentum. In that event, unless you open the throttle and gain some airspeed, you're going to come down again, pancakewise, with an undercarriage-wrecking thump, and receive the biggest surprise of your life.

One last word on landings. When in doubt, open the taps, overshoot, go round again and have another try. Like that, the worst you can end up with is a red face. Braving it through could get you an ignominious discharge from the Club, not to mention a private lawsuit for demolishing someone's greenhouse, pig-sty or home-built sauna cabin at the end of the runway.

SUMMARY

The Flying Syllabus for the PPL

The following is a list of flight and flight-related exercises which must be undertaken. Most are dual exercises, the remainder are handled solo.

1. Aircraft familiarization.
1E. Emergency drills.
2. Preparation for and action after flight.
3. Air experience.
4. Effects of the controls.
5. Taxi-ing.
5E. Emergencies.
6. Straight and level flight.
7. Climbing.
8. Descending.
9. Turning.
10. Stalling.
11. Spinning (not mandatory).
12. Take-off and climb to downwind position.
13. Circuits, approach and landing.
14. First solo flight.
15. Advanced turning (tight turns).
16. Operation at minimum level.
17. Forced landings – with and without power.
18. Pilot navigation.
19. Instrument appreciation.
20. Flight radiotelephony.

Each of these exercises will be entered in your logbook by your flying instructor as they are completed. Number 14 will probably be underlined in red – just as it ought to be. Additional remarks relating to emergency drills and cross-country solos will also be entered. The most coveted one, of course, is a rubber stamp headed 'Certificate of Test' which certifies satisfactory completion of the final handling test.

Continual Assessment Demands Continual Effort

The only way to progress in flying training is by making

consistent improvement, in both your flying and your ground training.

Your first solo depends on a tangible uniformity of circuit flying and landings. Arriving at your final handling test and the resultant licence is the product of displaying a depth of knowledge and a soundness of flying ability which remains stable day to day. Throughout your training, you will be watched, rated, assessed and, if up to the mark, promoted to the next stage. All you have to do is apply yourself.

5 Circuits

For some unaccountable reason, I look back on circuit-flying exercises – touch-and-go landings, that is – with a definite yearning.

In the circuit, you felt so completely safe. You were always within sight of the airfield and so, you thought, always home and dry. Round and round you went, your instructor by your side, bored absolutely wordless, his occasional yawn lulling you into a false sense of security until, as usual, you forgot some vital action or other, when he would become very animated indeed. By and large, though, all seemed very right with the world.

The appeal of circuit flying, as it happens, is certainly not universal. It takes different people different ways. Because of my special regard for low flying, I was thrilled to bits with it.

I should point out here and now that that illusion of invulnerability and safety is exactly that . . . an illusion. For one thing, you're flying a lot slower than normally, and at times you're not that many miles-an-hour away from stalling. Second, there are almost certainly other aircraft in the circuit with you (see Fig. 9). At a busy airfield – particularly one like mine where there are three clubs and an RAF university training establishment, plus an international air terminal – there could be half a dozen others up there doing exactly the same thing. At times, you tend to get pretty close to a few of them, which is an adventure that would be considered rather hazardous in any other circumstances.

As it happens, the only time I ever saw Jock completely lose his rag was during a circuit detail. We were turning gently onto base leg when we were unceremoniously 'cut up' and overtaken on the inside by an RAF Bulldog trainer. The pilot, obviously a novice, wanted to put his plane down on the ground first and was apparently prepared to go to any lengths

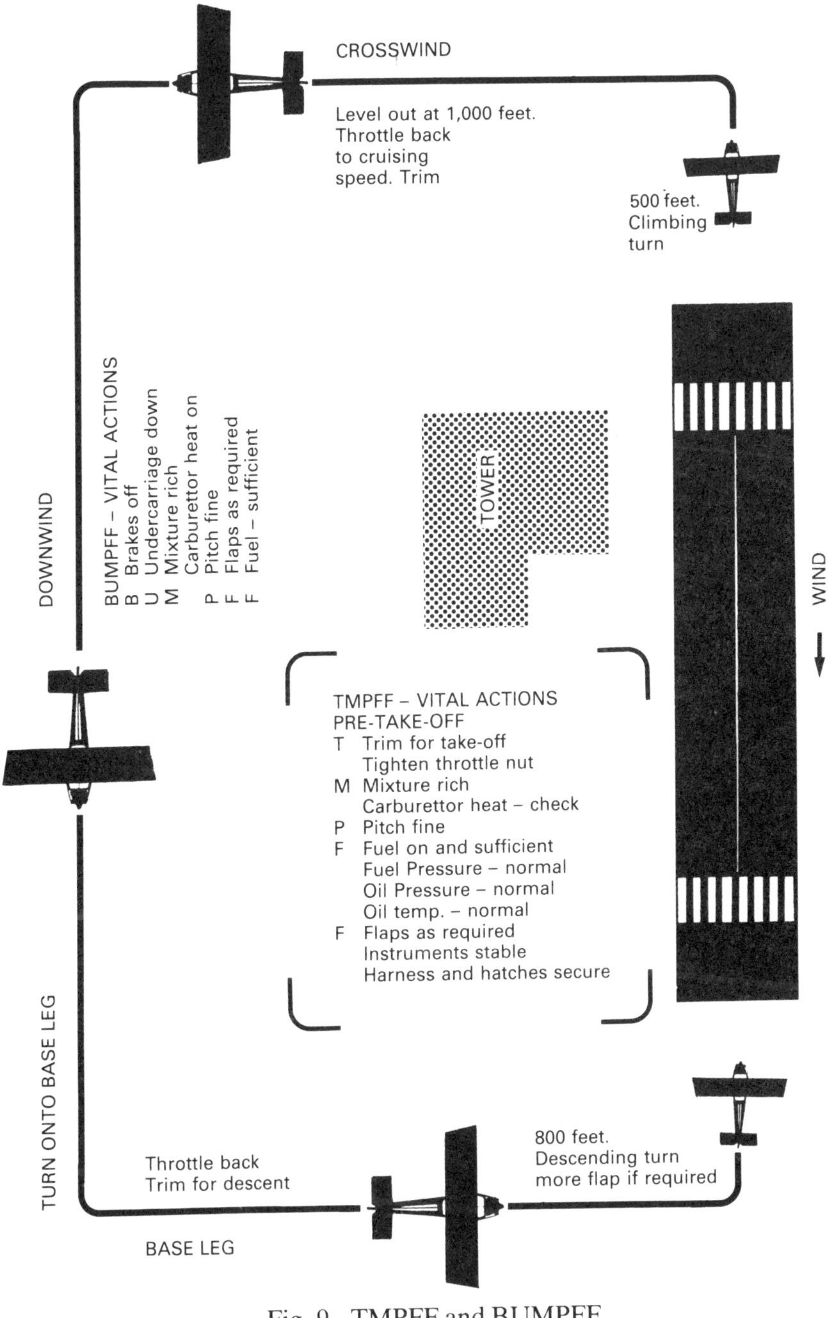

Fig. 9. TMPFF and BUMPFF

to achieve it – and this in spite of the fact that we had already been given ATC priority to turn onto finals. The air was bluish for a while in golf-uniform-foxtrot; and I must confess to being a little excited myself.

So if it's that much of a hassle, why bother to do it? The answer is simple: in the circuit you learn flying discipline. In the circuit, too, you get your first bash at the radio-telephone – which is also a discipline that after a while stops sounding like a foreign language and becomes a precise and concise dialogue.

CIRCUIT DRILL

First, let's accept we've told ATC what we're doing and have been given take-off permission. We are now climbing away from the runway at full throttle. At 500 feet we perform a climbing turn to the left. All circuits, unless specifically notified otherwise, are anticlockwise. If right-hand circuits are in force, you will be told either by r/t or by a red-and-yellow diagonally striped arrow in the airfield's signals area.

All right, we've banked left and are now on the crosswind leg. At 1,000 feet we drop the nose, throttle back to cruising speed and make the necessary trim adjustments. That's ATP – attitude, power, trim. (If we wanted to climb from level flight, it would be PAT: power, attitude, trim).

So far, so good, we are in the circuit – meaning that specified route everyone has to fly when approaching an airfield and desirous of landing thereon. Yes, there are other methods of approach: straight in onto finals, for example. You usually get that if there's no other traffic around. You can also join the circuit by connecting directly onto base leg. That one often happens when you're approaching from a direction opposite that which the circuit is being flown. By far the best rejoin, however, is the overhead version. It's shown opposite.

So we're flying straight and level. Craning over our left shoulder, we can see the runway just vacated. At the appropriate moment (my appropriate moment is when the end of the runway is just about to disappear beneath the aircraft's tail), we make a left turn without losing or gaining height. Here's where the hard work comes in. BUMPFF.

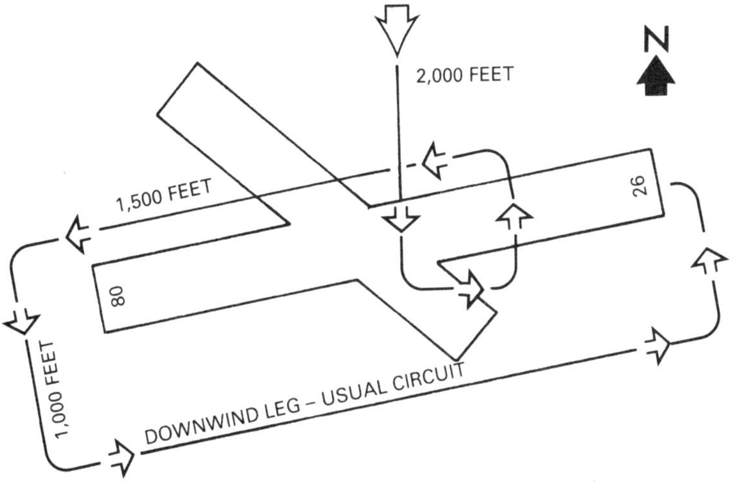

Fig. 10. The overhead rejoin. We wish to land on Runway 26.
1. Arrive overhead at 2,000 feet.
2. Orbit above 26 to check it's clear of other traffic.
3. Descend to 1,500 feet on the 'dead side' – the opposite side to that which the circuit is being flown.
4. Finally slot into the downwind leg at 1,000 feet, and continue the circuit as usual

Brakes off. We don't want our wheels locked when we land.

Undercarriage down – we shouldn't need to worry about that one if it isn't designed to retract!

Mixture rich and carburettor heat on.

Pitch. If you've got a variable pitch propeller, now's the time to find out how it works.

Flaps. Let's say ten degrees. That way we get the benefit of maximum lift and minimum drag.

Fuel. Here's where we discover that we forgot to check it before take-off. There must be enough, anyway, for an overshoot if necessary.

Wait for a break in radio transmissions, press the microphone tit and say: 'Golf-uniform-foxtrot . . . downwind.'

This will galvanize ATC to tell you: 'Golf-uniform-foxtrot, continue. Report turning base. You are number X to land two-six. Traffic information: an inbound Chipmunk joining from the ski-slope. Confirm you have contact.' Or words to that effect, meaning that you are in a queue state, that you must call before making your next left turn and that some awkward sod – the Chipmunk – is going to mess the queue up anyway by coming in from another direction.

Never mind all that. You'll learn to get used to it; you'll also learn that most pilots are gentlemen by design and will give right of way to anybody they may think is a little new or a little nervous.

Assuming that ATC tells you to turn base and doesn't keep you on the downwind leg until you reach the beach, you start throttling back to lose speed and height. Right now speed and height are critically important, and your angle of attack and revs are the key to both. Contrary to popular belief, the easiest way to lose height isn't to shove the stick hard forward. The most comfortable way, by far, is simply to pull the throttle out and give it less gas. Similarly, the best way to degrade forward speed when cruising is by raising the nose. Look at it this way, you've turned on to base leg and you want to descend from 1,000 to 800 feet . . . but gradually. All you have to do is ease the throttle back and hold the nose slightly up. Airspeed and height will drop off immediately. Now adjust the stick forward to find your glide slope, but prevent the angle of descent accumulating by holding it back a touch and retrimming for a perfect glide.

Practice and perseverance are what counts here, but in a while you will begin to 'feel' the aircraft into the right speed/glide attitude. A common fault in beginners, called 'chasing the airspeed' is a direct result of raising and lowering the nose intermittently in order to maintain that elusive airspeed.

Remarkably, my Cessna 150 had a 'sweetspot' similar in feel to that part of a golf club head which, when connecting with the ball, makes the shot effortless. It's that kind of sensation, and you'll know it for sure when you get it right.

And now the turn onto finals. Still losing height in that smooth glide – though not below 500 feet for safety – we bank to port and line up with the runway. Judging the final turn, especially in a good headwind or crosswind, also takes experience. The idea is to tee yourself up with the centre line of the runway and adopt the proper glide, via trim, for the final approach.

One thing worth remembering about that last turn is that you need never accept your initial attempt as irreversible. There's an easy way to readjust an 'oversteer' or 'understeer'. Quite simply, bank left or right the moment you realize the error, and this time straighten up on the centre line – bearing in mind that one of the reasons for the mistake in the first place was probably a crosswind, so you oversteer or understeer the correction turn accordingly.

A little harder to put right is too much or too little height on the final leg. If left uncorrected, the latter will result in a possible flying visit to the coalyard at the threshold of the runway. There are several ways, however, to save embarrassment and get down as originally intended.

When you're too high, you can take all the power off and drop the nose. But if you don't watch it, the airspeed will rise and you'll make an entrance at breakneck speed. Getting shot of that speed by holding the nose up will result in a touchdown three-quarters of the way along, or through the boundary fence of the runway. It takes a lot of skill in a too-high approach to run in, lose height and speed and still put her down on the numbers.

The next get-out is to sideslip, and that's the one I recommend. Sideslipping involves banking with ailerons only, say to the left, then applying a little *opposite* rudder to counteract the left turn. You'll be surprised how much height is lost, even in a mild sideslip. Obviously, the sideslip will put you left or right of the runway – because, as the word implies, you move sideways. To get back on course, you just sideslip the other way. Do remember, though, that speed increases in a sideslip, which means you must put some back pressure on the stick to hold the nose up and keep momentum from gaining, as explained earlier.

When you're too low, on the other hand, the logical thing to do is step on the juice and motor in – but be prepared to throttle back at the appropriate moment.

I've performed both these hilarious tricks on numerous occasions. In all certainty, so will you. Overshooting can be quite exhilarating, while undershooting seems to last interminably as you long-haul in just a few feet above the local scenery. Yes, we *know* full well the theory of getting properly set up on that final turn: correct height, correct speed, correct attitude. We even *know* where we go wrong the minute we go wrong. But the difference between know and do, as the man said, is like the difference between Brooklyn and Manhattan – you need some kind of bridge. That bridge, once again, is good old dedicated application.

THE FORCED LANDING

In addition to the foregoing, there's one other kind of circuit and landing you will have to master: the forced landing, the emergency landing.

Will you ever be called upon by the fates to perform one for real? In all probability you won't; aircraft are so well put together and so well monitored these days that airframe or engine failure is a several-million-to-one chance. But why be blasé? Isn't it a much better idea to take out some practical insurance against the eventuality? It certainly is; and the CAA agrees wholeheartedly so much so that they insist on emergency-landing procedures being taught as part of the PPL course.

Here are the basics of it. You're in mid-flight and suddenly you can't hear the engine any more. It has stopped, sparked its last plug, conned its last rod – for that trip anyway.

Immediately you become aware of this little problem, the first thing to do is stay calm. The second thing is to raise the nose and gain height with your excess forward speed. Now assume a shallow gliding attitude and trim for the glide. Have a good look around for a suitable field into which to put yourself safely. When I say field, you might care to try a newly completed section of an M-way, or a decent-sized though deserted car-park. But it must be somewhere that's free of livestock, empty of power lines, devoid of people . . . and close enough for you to reach.

While you're pondering this, work out the wind direction. You can do so (a) by remembering what it was at take-off and calculating accordingly, (b) by the movement of cloud and chimney smoke. If you're over water – God forbid –

wind direction can be assessed from the wind lanes on the surface.

When you're happy (and I can't think for one moment why you should be), make for the downwind edge of your chosen put-down spot. Now you're ready, if necessary, to turn onto base leg, and thus into wind for the landing.

At this point, start finding out why the engine failed. Check that the mixture is correctly set; that the mag switches and master switches have not been turned off inadvertently; that carburettor icing isn't the problem; that you in fact have fuel; and that the fuel cocks are on.

If everything checks out, you really do have a problem. So you must now make up your mind to go into the final approach. As you do so, switch everything off – not forgetting the fuel – apply flaps as required, check your seat harness, open the hatches, then get on the r/t as fast as you like with a nicely phrased Mayday call. That's always supposing you can unstick your tongue from the roof of your mouth! The rest depends on luck, judgement and a good hard prayer. Should it ever happen to you, and you feel like talking about it, do please get in touch and we'll have a pint on it.

In practising this exercise, the seriousness of the whole business will come starkly home. And the actual lengths you go to, in attempting to capture some realism, will be in direct proportion to your instructor's dedication – his belief, if you like, in the idea that, even if it is only an exercise, students should get as close to the real thing as he can push them.

Which is why it has been known for some instructors to stall the engine surreptitiously by pulling out the mixture lever, changing it from rich to weak. Even worse, I've heard that certain instructors will turn the fuel cock off in mid-flight, and then sit back and wait for the fun to begin.

Of course, Jock wouldn't do a thing like that. Not often, anyway.

Furthermore, a few instructors insist that you get to within a few feet of putting the aircraft down – an event causing quite a little surprise to the cows in the adjoining field. The farmer probably won't think much of it either.

But however involved your emergency exercises get, they're lessons well worth learning. So learn 'em.

What Jock did point out during one of these exercises, and which I pass on to you as very valuable information, is the following. When making an emergency landing without power, in some piece of spare pasture, it is far better to crash into the far fence at *ground speed*, than collide with the near fence at *flying speed*.

LANDING AWAY

At some time now – let's say you've put in six or seven hours – you'll be doing circuits like there's no tomorrow. Round and round you'll go as though connected to the ground by a control line. Lots of circuits means lots of landings. If you're very lucky, you'll get to do a few of these away from the home airfield. This not only rehearses you for the cross-country flights, and landings to come but also prevents your getting into the 'habit' of the home airfield. By that I mean that at the home airfield you make all your circuit turns on given landmarks – therefore your flying becomes mechanical; you're programmed to do certain things at a certain time, so there's very little skill and judgement.

My first landing at another airfield – at Glenrothes, in fact – was a mess. It's a single-strip field, with runway half the length and half the width of the one I'd become used to. A descent onto my home field *looked* like a descent – the tarmac got wider as I got nearer. At Glenrothes, however, the runway apparently stays exactly the same size from every height. And that's a little disconcerting for the novice.

The first attempt to get down resulted in a complete overshoot, and a bad one at that. My problem was that the plane started to drift to the right as soon as we crossed the threshold. It drifted so far that we were in real danger of demolishing the ATC hut some twenty yards off the runway. As I froze rigid on the controls, the hut came inexorably closer.

Jock was amazingly calm. 'Left rudder, open up and go round again.' Me, I just sat there, completely hypnotized by the prospect of impending, or so it seemed, doom.

'All right, I have control,' said this intrepid man; and he banged the throttle in and we roared away. 'You froze,' he said, stating the obvious. 'I don't want you to do that again. You understand?'

I nodded. How could I possibly guarantee it? 'Sorry,' I said. 'I really don't know what happened.'

'Let's try again, shall we.' It was an order, rather than a question. 'This time, try counteracting that drift with some rudder. Gently does it.'

The resultant landing was as good as I've ever made; and I turned at the end of the runway with a deftness, in such a confined area of tarmac, that surprised even Jock. We taxied to the fuelling point where a young overalled mechanic stood waiting. Part of the point of the exercise had been to land there for fuel.

So old jelly-knees here opened the hatch, leaned out and said: 'Five gallons of four-star, mate. And don't forget the stamps.'

The lad raised his eyes heavenward and directed his reply to Jock. 'Where d'you get him?' he asked. 'Out of a Lucky Bag?' He'd heard all the student-nervous jokes before.

While the tanks were being filled, Jock and I repaired to the ATC hut – presumably to apologize. Surprise, surprise! Alison Bailey, the beautiful lady who operates the ground-to-air radio service was all smiles. She was tact itself and gorgeous with it (and still is, by the way). When I blurted out my excuses for coming close to making her evacuate the place in a hurry, she adopted a sweet and understanding expression. 'I've seen worse – a lot worse.' And do you know, for a moment, I believed her. Which made me feel better – a lot better.

Just for fun, let's give you a reading from my personal log of about this time. It will prove, in the first place, that there really is one born every minute, and in the second place that, as badly as you may come to perform, you won't perform as badly as this.

HOUR SIX

Aggravated stalls. Very heavy handed on stick.

Two awful landings. Both at Glenrothes. Recommend a widening of the runway!

One mediocre landing at Edinburgh.

In club, met a fellow student about to take first lesson. He's a one-armed-bandit salesman. Noticed his coffee cup clattering in the saucer as his hands shook. I think someone's been talking to him about Jock!

HOUR SEVEN

Thirty minutes air exercises.

Thirty minutes touch-and-go landings.

'Touch-and-go' being the operative words!

Three reasonable circuits. But ATC are having trouble with my cockney accent. Must try to sound more refined. Maybe I should try: 'If I may be so bold, this is golf-uniform-foxtrot . . .'

Landings getting better. At least I'm now doing them alone. How Jock just sits there and watches it, I don't know!

HOUR EIGHT

Eight circuits. Nine landings. And one good one! Circuits becoming automatic. Have TMPFF and BUMPFF off to a tee.

Final approaches – no problem. But judging the round-out and hold-off seems to be getting more difficult. Obviously now run out of my share of beginner's luck!

Using landmarks on circuit religiously, i.e. twin tits of Pentland Hills. Maybury roundabout. Pigeon tower. If the local council moves either of the latter, I'm sunk!

About now, the prospect of soloing will be looming large in the mind and you want to do it with all your heart and soul. On the other hand, the imminence of it will frighten the living beejazus out of you. But because we're all made differently – luckily enough – some people will tend to show their apprehension more than others.

As a for-instance, I've watched fellow students fresh from their first lone flight in an attempt to gauge the aggro-quotient. It's similar to the way you inspect the patient who comes out of the dentist's chair just before you go in. One stiff-upper-lipped chap merely said 'Phew'! and left it at that. When it happened to me, all I wanted to do was break out the booze and tell everybody in sight just how clever I was. Which I did, on both counts.

I'd had the same feeling of euphoria on publishing my first book and becoming a dad for the first time. But then, fair do's, when I soloed, I *was* forty-six and a grandad to boot.

Even more wonderfully, my wife was at the club the day I winged, unaccompanied, over unsuspecting Edinburgh. Better still, she was listening to my every deathless syllable on the r/t.

It was a superb experience, and one I relive at the drop of a hat. Don Quixote was up there charging at windmills, while Dulcinea was on the deck watching.

SUMMARY

Vital Actions Prior to Landing

B. Brakes off.
U. Undercarriage down.
M. Mixture rich. Carburettor heat on.
P. Pitch.
F. Flaps. As required.
F. Fuel. On and sufficient.

In the circuit, these vital actions are completed on the downwind leg. On completion, call the tower and notify them of your downwind position.

The correct terminology for an aborted landing is a 'go-round'. The word 'overshoot' is no longer correct currency and is used by pilots only in conversation among themselves.

Setting Up The Correct Attitude on The Landing Approach.

(a) Lose height by closing the throttle.
(b) Degrade forward speed by pulling back the stick and raising the nose of the aircraft.
(c) Maintain a constant glide-slope by use of the trim-tab.
(d) Maintain a constant approach speed (determined by aircraft type) using (a), (b) and (c) above.

Actions To Be Taken After Engine Failure In Flight

(i) Raise the nose to gain height with the excess forward speed.

(ii) Gently lower the nose and trim for a shallow glide.
(iii) Locate a suitable landing site.
(iv) Determine wind direction.
(v) Proceed to the downwind edge of your proposed landing site.
(vi) Turn crosswind, then on the base leg to make your approach as normal.

During steps (v) and (vi), try to establish why the engine has failed. Check that the mixture is correctly set; that magneto switches are on; apply carburettor heat; and establish your fuel state. If all fails, make the appropriate emergency radio transmission.

6 Solo!

Not unremarkably, all that the majority of students want to do is go solo. Doing so marks you out from the rest, sets you head and shoulders above the mob. Your entire attitude to life in general changes. Like you hear yourself saying: 'Who does that bloke in the car behind think he's hooting? *I* can fly aeroplanes!' You come to realize, however, that soloing isn't the be all and the end all – in truth, it's only the beginning. But what do you care at the time? You don't know and you don't want to know. Say no more: the solo is the thing to aim for; it's the stepping-stone between complete and utter novice to reasonably competent flyer.

And one thing's for sure: you'll remember the event for the rest of your life. I've met people who can recall it graphically, second by second, even though the enterprise was carried out thirty, forty, even fifty years ago. One man says he sang all the way round the circuit – that the tune was called 'Where Did You Get That Hat?', which was current *circa* 1919, only goes to prove the total memorability of the event. As for me, I sweated and lit a cigarette every thirty seconds. Both ashtrays were jammed by the time I reached base leg; and the performance to extinguish them all before turning finals would have won Oscars for Laurel and Hardy.

Here's the way it was.

11 June happened to be a glorious day, with no cloud and little wind – which, for Scotland, is a rare event, comparable, perhaps, with stumbling across the Holy Grail at a junkshop in the Portobello Road. Anyway, an early morning trip was definitely on the cards, so we took full advantage and carried out nine circuits. Afterwards, in the flight office, Jock made the appropriate entry in his log sheets.

'Why don't you come back after lunch,' he said with a half-grin. 'Say 2.30?'

'For . . . er . . . for what exactly?'

'Oh, I don't know. I'm sure we'll think of something.'

Instinct told me I'd arrived, but I didn't want to press the terror button until I was 400 per cent positive.

'Let me put it this way,' I said. 'Will I be doing more circuits?'

'Yes, yes, circuits will certainly be involved. But in the interim, no lager and lime.'

Well, a nod's as good as a wink; and the no-drinking rule spoke volumes.

'You have my word,' I said, and added. 'May I bring Marion?'

'By all means. I'm sure she appreciates a good laugh . . . same as the rest of us.'

I drove back to the office and told my wife that I was expected back at the club for a special exercise. I omitted to mention my suspicions, since I wanted the solo – if solo it was to be – to come as a complete surprise, wanted her to get as much of a kick out of it as I would. It goes without saying, though, that she smelled a great big rat when I confided that I didn't fancy a lunchtime pint.

Thus, after a sausage roll and (I don't believe this) a glass of milk, we motored out to the airport.

'We'll do a couple of circuits,' Jock told me on arrival. 'Let's just hope the touchdowns haven't deteriorated since this morning.'

So we did that couple of circuits – one touch-and-go, one dead stop. As we taxied back to the apron, Jock unhooked the mike.

'Edinburgh tower, this is golf-uniform-foxtrot. Are you willing to accept a solo at this time?'

I crossed my fingers, crossed my legs and everything else that it was physically possible to cross, willing the ATC to come back with a great big no.

After a wait of at least ten seconds – the longest ten seconds of my life – the reply came flooding over the speaker.

'Affirmative, uniform-foxtrot. Proceed in your own time.'

Had I heard correctly? Was this it? Oh, blimey! Oh, help! Oh, you unbelievable wally! What in the name of all that's sensible was I doing here?

But wait a minute, pal, I'm not feeling all that well. As a matter of fact, I think I'm about to experience a massive coronary. There you are, I was right, my heart has stopped.

Now let's be adult about this. How could you possibly allow someone of my undoubted mental instability to take your very expensive aeroplane into the sky?

Apart from anything else, I don't know whether you noticed it, but the ammeter is showing a discharge. I've been meaning to report it for weeks; and you must agree that the engine is running decidedly rough. Let's be honest: it's about time a good mechanic had a look at this crate. And he'd have a field day – a fortnight should be enough time to pin down all the faults.

Yet, it was inevitable. I imagine I could have given a categoric refusal, but that would have been unutterably cowardly – characteristic, but unutterably cowardly.

'Do you think I'm up to it?' I asked, hoping like mad that he would give it a second thought.

Jock smiled that languid smile. 'If you're not and you have a leg left unbroken when you land, *I'll* break it.'

Quickly, he briefed me on the r/t calls and responses to make and expect. He also rattled through the vital actions, circuit heights and landmarks.

'By the way,' he said, 'you know what to do in the event of engine failure on take-off, don't you?'

'Drop the nose,' I replied, 'and find a landing spot 60° forward.'

'Correct. But try not to make it the terminal car-park, eh?'

With a thumbs up he was gone – and so was my bottle. I felt very alone. A plague victim couldn't have experienced greater isolation.

'CLEAR FOR TAKE-OFF'

I re-started the engine and performed all the checks. This was it; there was no going back now. I operated the rudder pedals. They were amazingly easy to manipulate. Obviously, the man kept his feet on them when we were flying. Who could blame him?

Apart from a few fluffs, I handled the r/t moderately well –

pretty good going for someone with a mouth full of sand. At this stage, Marion was listening in on Jock's short-wave receiver, he having nipped back to switch on and give everyone the benefit of my discomfiture. Later, her verdict was that I sounded quite nervous. The 'quite' surprised me, but she was always the mistress of the under-statement. I remember her once describing Mohammed Ali as 'not a bad boxer'.

Eventually I managed to steer uniform-foxtrot onto the runway. In retrospect, I swear that that dear little plane did it completely unaided. While I was holding, waiting for permission to go, I saw vehicles in the distance. They came closer, and through eyes glazed with sweat I saw that they were fire-engines – and they were for me.

Nobody had told me this, but I learned subsequently that every first-solo artist in Edinburgh gets them. Just in case. I figured they were all on overtime anyway and they'd be delighted to pick up some extra money from working on a good bonfire. There is no truth, I'm glad to say, in the rumour that the local scrap merchant is also called in on these occasions.

'Golf-uniform-foxtrot. You are clear for take-off.'

I fumbled with the mike and acknowledged the signal to go. What I really wanted to do was read them my last will and testament, followed by the Agincourt speech from *Henry V*, with Portia's fifteen-minute oration as an encore, just to delay things; also to prove once and for all that I was indeed certifiable and no fit person to be bashing aircraft around the sky.

Instead, I thought: 'Come on, Paddy – for once in your life do it right.'

'Oh, very well,' I replied aloud; and banged the throttle right home.

HOW LIGHT SHE FEELS

The 150 fairly skipped down the runway, its rapid acceleration and lightness of feel coming as quite a shock. It shouldn't have, because when Jock had left the plane, we'd lost half, more than half, our payload. She came unstuck before I realized what was happening. Up, up, up went the nose – too high. I shoved the stick forward – too hard. Down, down, down. Pull back, keep her climbing; she was pitching like something out of the Americas Cup.

But I was airborne and that was the main thing. With which, the starkest of all thoughts hit me right between the eyes. I was up, but could I actually get the bloody thing down again – and on its wheels for preference? Then, literally out of the blue, Jock's wisdom of past days came shining through, and I performed two of the most vital actions of my life. I trimmed for the climb and lit a cigarette.

Someone once said that the prospect of being hanged in the morning concentrates the mind wonderfully. It's true.

I started getting my act together. I suddenly felt calm – sweaty but calm. Turning crosswind, then downwind, I did everything I'd been taught – the drills, the ATC calls. At that moment, walking on water would have been a minor miracle. *This* was what it was all about. The elation, the absolute power *erupting* absolutely, that glorious sensation from realizing you are fulfilling a life's ambition. I was up there with all the Spitfires of my young days, sun glinting on wings, engines screaming; and now I knew what it meant to fly, really to fly. Bring on the Messerschmitts!

Forgetting the first cigarette, which was smouldering away in the ashtray, I lit another. Dirty rhymes issued from my mouth like incantations to ward off any evil spirits which might be waiting to pounce. Eskimo Nell was violently interrupted by a stentorian squawk from the r/t. 'Say again,' I said, having missed every syllable. Were they, I wondered, all crammed at the tower windows and taking bets on the precise position where the crash would occur?

Not a bit of it. A carefully enunciated message from a gentle voice told me merely that I was alone in the circuit and clear to land any time I felt like it. Alone was right – it made good sense to stay a long way away for the next few minutes.

'You're a pal,' I offered, departing from the regulation wording. I've never yet learned to communicate with ATC and not say please or thank you. Sometimes, though not often, they respond in kind. One charming fellow, upon being thanked for his assistance, told me: 'That's what we're here for, sir.' You'll agree that that kind of attitude is most reassuring, particularly to the novice. While I'm not advocating the holding of turgid discourses over the air, since that would defeat the whole object of accuracy through brevity, the odd pleasantry certainly seems to help everyone relax.

So there I was on base leg, and all was right with the world. A swift glance at the tower showed me they weren't evacuating the place of everything movable – a good sign. But little did they know how close I was to helping them in their long and tedious fight for new premises! Beneath me, the landmark for turning base arrived and I banked sharply to the left. It was a tight turn, a jack-the-lad turn, and altogether too over-the-top for my taste. I quickly levelled the wings; being overly adventurous on one's first solo outing was asking for trouble.

Out of the corner of my mouth, I gave ATC the benefit of my position in a lazy drawl. They, in turn, gave me more rope. Come on in, they invited, in not so many words, and I aimed the aircraft at the runway centre line.

THE MOMENT OF TRUTH

Right about then, the cocky façade I'd erected on the way round disintegrated like meringue in a rainstorm. The bravado upped and went. Here it was, the moment of truth; and there, if I made a mistake, was the prospect of coal-black infinity, stretching as far ahead as the mind could comprehend. Was this the end of civilization as I knew it? Would half a dozen people shortly be carrying me by the handles?

'Right, Paddy,' I confided, hastily stubbing the fags out. 'I'm only going to show you this the once.'

I am of the opinion that golf-uniform-foxtrot landed herself. Agreed, the round-out came too early, the float along the runway was overlong, and she slapped the undercarriage down somewhat sharply, but she stuck and stayed stuck. The rest, as they say, was easy.

Jock was waiting on the apron; he seemed quite happy as I taxied in. I switched off and climbed out.

The wind felt sharp and I realized I was bathed head to foot in perspiration. I made a mental note to switch off the cabin heat before the next trip.

Jock was all smiles when I grabbed his hand and pumped his arm. 'Did you see that?' I asked. 'I don't believe it, I just don't believe it,' I repeated over and over. 'Did *I* do that?'

My instructor, who has seen it all and done it all – not the very least of which was the saving of the life of HM King Hussein in a Middle East air battle; and I hope he'll let me write the story one day – my instructor, who has seen it all, was thoroughly delighted.

That went for me, also.

You won't be surprised to discover that we adjourned to the bar forthwith, where I proceeded to get stuck into the mixture as before.

While the circumstances of my solo failed to make the national Press, and even missed mention on *News at Ten*, it was momentous for me.

As it will be for you. For ever and ever, amen.

A word, here, about the way instructors work *vis-à-vis* soloing. No matter how many hours you put in before the solo, the event always seems to come as a complete surprise. In other words, very few people have any precognition that it's about to happen. So nine times out of ten, the instructor hits the student with the issue completely uncued and unannounced. He does that for a couple of reasons.

(1) A student who has been lying awake all the previous night, worrying about the prospect of going alone, will definitely not be at his brightest-eyed and bushiest-tailed for the job.

(2) Instructors like to spring it on you so that they can have the pleasure of watching your face change from happy-go-lucky to out-and-out dementia in one second flat. It's called sadism – they all revel in it. How do you think they got the job in the first place? It's one of the qualifications.

SUMMARY

Actions to be Taken after Engine Failure on Take-off

(i) Drop the nose. If you are still above the runway, try to regain it.
(ii) Otherwise, trim for a shallow glide.

(iii) Locate a landing site at no greater angle than 60° forward of your line of vision.
(iv) If you have time, attempt to locate the engine fault and make an emergency radio transmission.

Never, ever attempt to turn back to the airfield – you almost certainly won't make it.

Although your first solo flight will be numbered among the most momentous experiences of your life, it is only the beginning. The first milestone on a very long road.

It is, nonetheless, a magical moment. And I think those clubs which neglect to award a set of wings, or at least some kind of certificate, just to mark the occasion, are doing their students a grave disservice.

7 Building the Hours

From here on it gets more and more challenging, but also more and more interesting. The sessions of solo circuits first, and then those initial hesitant steps out of the circuit into unrestricted airspace alone are truly emboldening. However, you won't be allowed that kind of rein until you have a fair grasp of instrument work, navigation work and advanced aircraft handling – three diverse ingredients which together inject some precision into your flying. You already have the discipline; now for the airmanship.

In the early hours, you'll come away with the distinct impression that the aeroplane somehow has a mind of its own and tends to go wandering off anywhere it fancies. Later, however, when you discover the thoroughly enjoyable art of course-keeping and when, if you're lucky, you get the chance to fly in cloud using instruments only, the plane will concede to your mastery.

It's a laugh a minute at the start, you understand – just nothing goes right. But mistakes are there to be learned from; and if you make enough, you'll learn a lot. I could give you a dozen examples, but one should suffice right now.

INSTRUMENT FLYING

Around about my eleventh hour, at a time when I was beginning to believe I knew everything there was to know about flying (well, hadn't I performed sixteen solo circuits?), Jock decided we should have a go at instrument flying.

Normally this exercise is conducted on a clear day with the student wearing a visor, a kind of helmet which prevents his making any visual reference to the ground or the horizon and restricts his vision to the cabin instruments only. Thus he flies, as it were, blind. The day in question, I confess, was no normal day in every sense of the word. The sky was as black as your hat, six-eighths cloud at 3,000 feet, and a wind fit to half you. Even the birds were grounded.

'Just what we need,' said Jock, as we climbed straight into the muck. 'You'll enjoy this.' He failed to add: 'Not a lot,' but should have.

It was like being entombed in a great wad of grey cotton-wool. This was my first experience of flying a light aircraft in cloud and I vowed there and then it would be my only one. Famous last words: he had me up there, at different times, for four hours in all – the mandatory hours for a PPL. In the event, I'm glad he did. At least, if I'm ever caught napping by a swift closing-in of weather, I'll be proficient enough to keep us safely airborne and fly out of trouble.

Jock pointed to the direction indicator. 'You're flying on a heading of zero-eight-zero, OK? Now change heading and steer two-seven-zero.'

There was a long pause while I worked out where two-seven-zero was on the dial. There was an even longer pause while I made up my mind which way to turn to reach it.

Now, it doesn't take a genius to work out that the difference between zero-eight-zero and two-seven-zero is exactly 190°. Furthermore, it doesn't have to be calculated because there it is in front of you on the instrument panel plain as daylight. A left turn due west is all that's required.

Here's where the trouble started; and right off the bat I made two classic mistakes. When an aircraft turns left, the direction indicator revolves right, or clockwise, and vice versa. So whichever way you turn, the dial comes round to meet you from the opposite direction of the turn. It's really very simple. Only a twit could be so thoroughly disoriented as to get it wrong. Anyway, I turned right!

Realizing the fluff, because I was now going away from two-seven-zero, and not wanting to appear even more dense than already established, I applied hard left rudder and hard left stick. Thereby hung the second classic mistake.

With no outside horizon to determine the attitude of the plane, down went the nose; and, unbeknown to me, it dropped farther and farther as the turn accumulated. Believably, I was too engrossed waiting for due west to appear on the datum line to notice what was happening.

Long before we reached the appointed heading, the plane broke through the cloud at a very odd angle, indeed – serving to give me the shock of my life. We were heading for the ground, in no uncertain terms, in a tight spiral dive.

Four-letter words ricocheted around the cockpit, and they were all fired by me.

'Well, what do you propose doing about it?' queried Jock, with all the nonchalance of the breed.

'Straighten her out?' I asked. It was a tentative enquiry, but what a ridiculous thing to say. In mitigation, however, you have to look at it from my point of view: he still wanted two-seven-zero and in my bemused state I couldn't work out which was the most important: our altitude or our course.

I recovered the aircraft in good time, but put a lot of 'g' on us in the attempt.

'How the hell did I manage that?' I wondered. 'I don't normally get into that kind of mess.'

Jock was mildly sympathetic. 'First of all,' he said, 'your turn was far too aggressive and the bank too steep. You can get away with it in the clear, because your eyes are telling you exactly how you're positioned in relation to fixed objects. But in cloud, there's nothing to latch onto. Secondly, you weren't paying enough attention to the artificial horizon; and even when you were, you wouldn't believe what it said. Never, ever rely on your own sense of balance in that kind of situation. It will let you down every time.' He indicated the instruments. 'These are the only things you can trust.'

After a while, I learned to disregard my own senses; but I'll tell you here and now it was very difficult. Even flying straight and level in cloud takes a bit of doing at first. Your own equilibrium tells you one thing, the instruments tell you something else. In those circumstances always take the word of the machinery. Incidentally, you will feel quite shattered after these exercises – they say that everybody does. I reckon the concentration involved would levitate tables!

As for that turn, it should have been what's called a rate-one turn. In a Cessna 150 it works out at about 15° or 16° of bank at an approximate airspeed of some 95 mph.

TIGHT TURNS

Advanced turning exercises are something else again. They are designed to produce the tightest possible turns without losing or gaining altitude and without stalling. Execution is relatively simple once you get the hang of it; and similarly with the physical sensation once you get the idea of going *with* the aircraft, rather than trying to hold yourself upright. (In this sort of turn, your body is going to be as near as dammit parallel with the ground.) You enter the turn as normal, but keep the bank full on instead of half-steering against it as you would in a regular turn. It's all or nothing, this one. In a left turn you hold the stick well back, keeping the nose plumb on the now spinning horizon. In a right-hand turn the only difference is that you hold the stick forward for the same result. Why? It's all due to the torque of the engine and its inclination to pull to the right. More than that I'm not qualified to say, though it will be fully covered in your ground training.

So, having batted around in the clouds for almost an hour, it crossed my mind to ask where we were. Jock put his tongue firmly into his cheek. 'We could go down and find out,' he said. 'Better still, let's ask ATC to locate us on radar.' He called them up and they obliged.

Even more interesting was his request for radar assistance back to the airfield – which they also agreed to. The result was a most rewarding ten minutes, graphically proving the undoubted benefits of flying from a well-equipped major airport. They assisted us, with full altitude and heading instructions, to within a mile of the runway threshold; and it turned out to be the runway used by the largest aircraft currently in service: it's around 2,500 metres long. After landing, it took us some considerable time to taxi to the nearest exit point, rather like landing on the M1 midway between junctions.

You may or, indeed, may not have heard of a charge called a landing fee. Landing fees are dues levied by the airfield's owners or operators upon the flying club and, in turn, upon the student pilot. The cash is payable for every single landing, so it tends to make circuit work a little bit pricey. Most airfields, I'm happy to say, charge only a nominal fee of a few (and I mean a few) pounds. There is a minority, however, that sting you for astronomical sums. The answer is to give the aforementioned highwaymen a miss until they get some sense. I thought I'd better tell you, anyhow, before you got yourself into something requiring a bank loan to get out of.

BASIC NAVIGATION

Around about now, navigation will begin to rear its interesting head; and if navigation is to you what navigation was to me, a ten-letter word, here are some pointers to get you started.

Assuming you can keep a course – that's maintain the aircraft fairly steadily on a predetermined heading (and until you can, all the navigation in the world will be totally pointless), you'll want to know how to plot a course that gets you accurately from A to B.

There's quite a bit to take in here, so we'll progress slowly. The first ingredient to absorb is CDMVT which stands for Compass. Deviation. Magnetic. Variation. True. You can remember it by the mnemonic 'Cadbury's Dairy Milk Very Tasty' or 'Can't Do My Velocity Triangles'. Take your pick, but make it stick; it's crucial.

Compass is exactly what it says: the compass bearing in degrees from A to B. Now it's a fact that compasses suffer from a complaint called deviation. They pick it up from the metal parts and electrical bits that go to make up an aircraft. Deviation, then, is the figure in degrees by which a compass is being interfered with and by which it must be corrected on site. Every aircraft has its own deviation value, and this will be displayed in the aircraft. For practical purposes, you'll never need bother about it, but for reasons of passing exams, you must know what deviation is; and that happens to be the whole idea behind this diatribe.

Magnetic next. Simply, it's the compass reading you end up with after correcting for deviation. Would you believe it, though, it still has faults, because the compass needle points to magnetic north, not true north. Magnetic north is actually somewhere in Canada, so attempting to travel accurately due north solely on a compass reading is a waste of time – you'd be miles out. What's worse, magnetic north changes by the hour, since it circumnavigates the pole on a permanent basis.

So wherever you stand on the globe, true north and magnetic north are never comparable. Don't ask me why. I came along several million years after the place was built.

For the conducting of navigation, at any rate, we can soon put things to rights. We do so by compensating in our calculations for this anomaly; and the anomaly is called variation. Take a look at any aviation chart and you'll see the variation figure clearly marked – it's written in the map legend as a line of equal magnetic variation. Currently, the variation figure for Skegness, for example, is 6° west. At Edinburgh it's 8° west.

One to go, and that's True. This being the heading (the track on your map) from which the D, M and V variables are computed.

How do we arrive at it? Just read this.

Deviation east – Compass least.
Deviation west – Compass best.
Variation east – Magnetic least.
Variation west – Magnetic best.

Now to put it into practice, using our Deviation/Variation rhyme. Given a Compass bearing of 090°, where Deviation is 2° E, what is Magnetic?

C	D	M	V	T
090°	2° E	?		

It's 092°. Deviation east. Compass least – less than Magnetic. So 090° + 2° = 092°. Were we now to employ a Variation figure of 5°E, what would be True?

C	D	M	V	T
090°	2° E	092°	5° E	?

Variation east, Magnetic least – less than True. Thus 092° + 5° = 097°.

Here's another. The Compass bearing is 180° with Deviation of 2° E. Further, the Magnetic heading is 182° with a Variation figure of 8° W. What is our True heading?

C	D	M	V	T
180°	2° E	182°	8° W	?

Deviation East, Compass least. Variation West, Magnetic best, i.e. better than True.

Without too much cerebral steam, we obviously come up with 174°. Eureka! In fact, you need only three of the constituents to find the remaining two. Like this:

C	D	M	V	T
150°	2° E	?	8°W	?

The answer is 152° (M) and 144° (T). You'll be given questions along these lines in your exam, so it's imperative you know the rules. The reason I've gone on about it at length is that some people – including some very bright people – develop a mental block over it. In my case, it was more a mental breakdown, involving days of hair-tearing on my part and minutes of exasperation on Jock's.

WIND AND DRIFT

It's true to say that, but for wind, navigation would be easier than stirring tea. Trouble is, it's everywhere, and the whole world is influenced by it one way or another. Wind occurs when there are variations in atmospheric pressure over the earth's surface – though that isn't our concern right now. Our problem is to know how to compensate for it in flight. One of the first principles to grasp is the difference between airspeed and groundspeed. There *is* a difference, and it's called 'wind effect'.

I explained in Chapter 3 that the airspeed indicator (ASI) is served by the pitot head: a slim tube usually slung from the leading edge of the wing or, in many experimental jets, straight out from the nose. The pitot head constantly samples and measures the force of air flowing into it, recording it on the dial of the ASI. Consequently, an indicated airspeed (IAS) determines the speed of an aircraft *through the air* – not over the ground.

Imagine we're flying in a dead calm at an IAS of 100 knots. Groundspeed in this instance, logically, will also be 100 knots.

Suddenly a 30-knot wind springs up, hitting us on the nose directly fore and aft. As you might expect, this half gale slows us down somewhat. In fact, it slows us down by some 30 knots, giving a groundspeed of around 70 knots. Yet the ASI continues to read 100 knots, simply because that's our speed through the air *plus* the speed of the wind colliding with us.

Conversely, if the 30-knot wind happened to be coming in from directly astern, we'd be shoved along by the same amount, and both airspeed and groundspeed would rise to 130 knots.

Which is all well and good and easily calculated, but the wind is fickle – it blows from all directions. Accordingly, a wind arriving sideways on – let's say at 45° to our line of flight – will not only slow the plane down but push it 45° off course into the bargain. The push is called drift, and if we neglect to compensate for same, it will take us miles off the proposed course.

Consider wanting to fly from A to B with a wind as shown: unless some allowance is made for drift, you'll arrive over C more than slightly late for your appointment at B.

With this in mind (see Fig. 12.), the allowance to be made and the course to be steered is D – for, in aiming for D, you'll drift to B, which is exactly where you wanted to get. To put it into textbook language, A to B is your Track Required and A to D your True Heading.

However, do bear in mind that, although your heading is

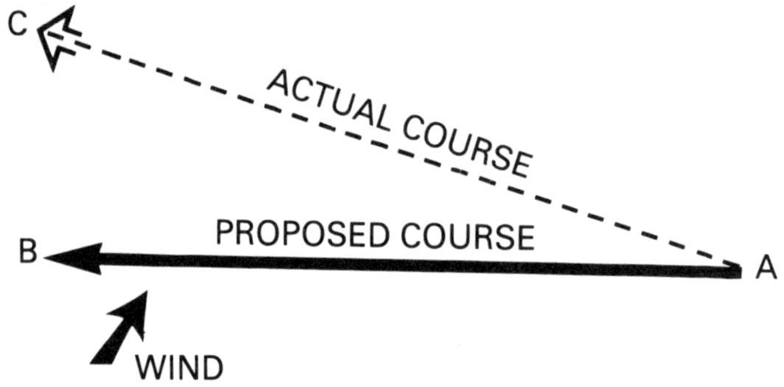

Fig. 11. Actual course and proposed course

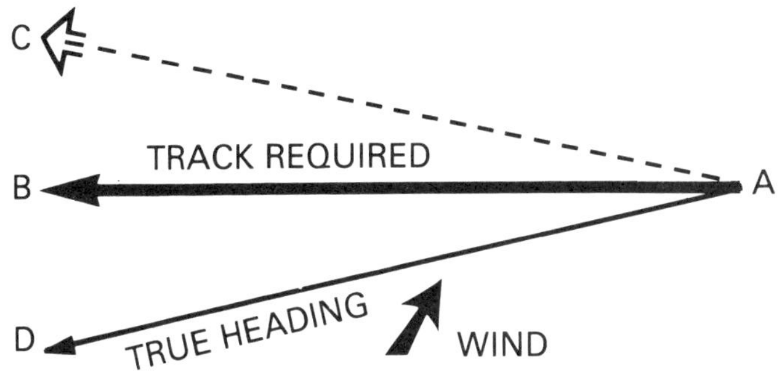

Fig. 12. Track required and true heading

set as A to D, your actual course over the ground will be straight along the Track Required, on account of the fact that the wind has an effect on you from the moment of leaving A.

The calculations which have to be made are similar to those when aiming off for wind in target shooting. How do you make them? You've guessed it: with a triangle of velocities. Don't let's get too complicated; that would defeat the object of this book. A simple example, though, should be acceptable. (see Fig. 13.)

We want to fly from X to Y, a distance of fifty nautical miles, on a track required of 270° – that's due east to due west. We're told before we go to expect a wind *from* 360° at a velocity of 30 knots. Given that our aircraft cruises at 90 knots – the True Airspeed (TAS) – we can now work out the necessary triangle of velocities and find our true heading.

Grab a sheet of paper and a ruler and draw the X to Y track. Make it any length you wish within reason; if you're working in millimetres, 150 will do, but do stick to millimetres throughout. Now draw in a wind velocity line – it's coming from 360°, which is due north and a convenient right angle. On this line mark off the 30-knot wind velocity from the Y destination point and call it Z. Finally, put the ruler on Z and intersect the track line at exactly 90 knots. Call that A.

To determine the true heading, simply put a protractor on the angle at A. It's 289°. (An ordinary school protractor will work, but the proper tool is an Airtour navigation protractor. If you take up flying seriously, you'll certainly need one.)

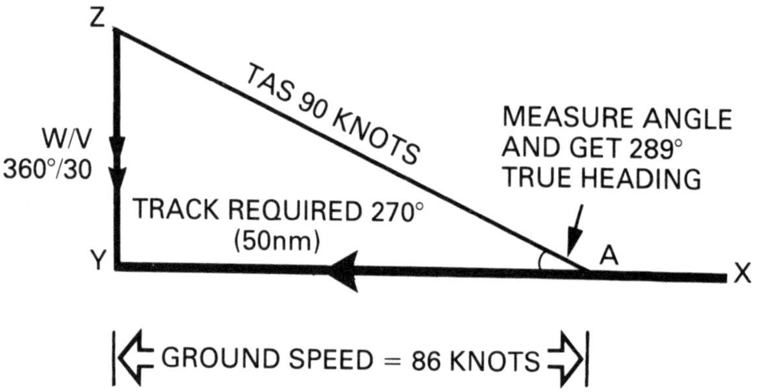

Fig. 13. Determining the true heading

With the triangle of velocities, you can also calculate groundspeed. Just measure the line Y to A and get 86 knots.

In practice, the triangle of velocities would be translated onto an aviation chart, at which time you'd see the actual X to Y course, with the landmarks, towns etc. along it and over which you will fly, the true heading of 289° to be steered, and the groundspeed of 86 knots.

This method has been largely superseded by an instrument called an Airtour computer. It's a kind of circular slide-rule that does everything bar select eight score-draws for the coupon. The computer can handle simple problems like the above in seconds, while similar tasks of calculating fuel consumption and fuel remaining, making temperature and weight conversions, and questions on time and distance, can be answered in short order. It's worth its weight in gold but costs only a few pounds; you'll be more than glad you invested in one.

With the computer, you need draw only one line on the map: the track required. Once you have the bearing of that, the computer does the rest. The only other considerations are the application of Deviation and the adding or subtracting of Variation to the result (this goes for the triangulated result, too) and you're off and running.

The mathematicians among you will realize that the figures

given in our example can also be used to calculate the time the flight will take. Like this:

$$\frac{\text{Distance}}{\text{Groundspeed}} = \frac{50}{86} \times \frac{60}{1} = 35 \text{ minutes.}$$

I propose to look at just one more element in the navigation scheme of things: the one-in-sixty rule. This is the solution to all your navigation errors while in flight.

For instance, there you are, bombing along on what you think is a correct heading, and you've covered about thirty miles with a further forty to go, when below your left wing up tips a landmark which shouldn't be there. It should, according to your map, be five miles to the north. What has almost certainly happened in this case – assuming you held a good course – is that a change in wind direction has caused you to drift off track.

No good shouting for your instructor: he's either in the clubhouse relieving other students of 50p a time over games of pool, at which pastime he is an acknowledged master, or he's in the bar chatting up the air hostesses. Instead, invoke the one-in-sixty rule; and the rule says this: if an aircraft has flown sixty miles and is known to be one mile off track, it has a track error of one degree.

To relate the rule to our dilemma above, bearing in mind that the proportion is always 1:60, our five-mile track error after thirty miles looks like this:

$$\frac{5}{30} \times \frac{60}{1} = 10° \text{ track error}$$

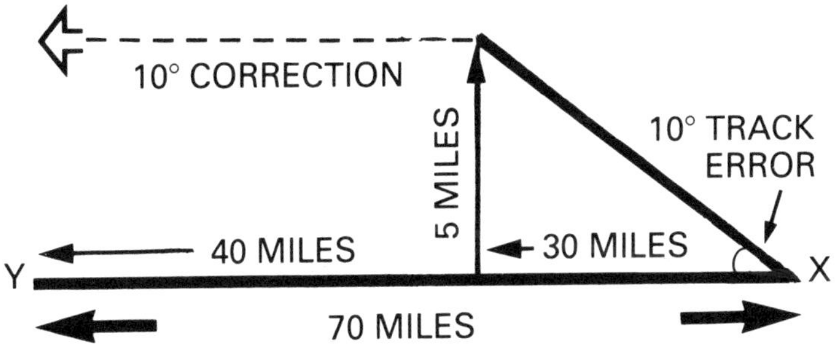

Fig. 14. Track error

Were we to alter course by only 10°, in the hope of getting back on track, we would actually never get back. In fact, we'd simply fly parallel to the track at a distance of five miles.

What we must now take into account is the distance remaining to fly, and how to fly it without further mistake. So we make the same kind of one-in-sixty calculation with the remaining distance, as before, and add both figures together. With forty miles to go and a track error of 10°, or five miles, the equation looks like:

$$\frac{5}{40} \times \frac{60}{1} = 7\tfrac{1}{2}^\circ$$

Now add that 7½° to the earlier 10° and the answer is 17½° – which is the heading correction we must make to hit the destination on the button.

These simple calculations are well worth becoming familiar with. There are few things worse than being adrift, aloft alone, with your computer neatly packed in a briefcase at the back of the plane and ungettatable. You'll really wish you knew the one-in-sixty rule – I can almost guarantee it.

CROSS-COUNTRY

As soon as you have a working knowledge of navigation, plus a modicum of air law and meteorology besides, your instructor will put you onto solo cross-country flights. They begin gently, with trips of sixty minutes or so. Their purpose is to

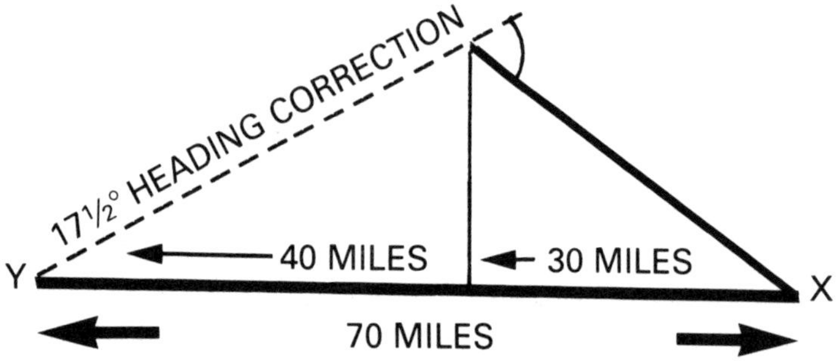

Fig. 15. Heading correction

give you experience of course-keeping, map-reading and the flight-timing of individual legs along the route. Gradually, the flight duration will increase – as will your confidence. You'll steer to two or three given reference points, towns, large lakes or headlands, some thirty miles from base; and when you happen to stumble upon those points, at approximately the estimated time, there will be jubilation in the cockpit and much relief in your heart.

During each of my cross-country runs, I invariably grew tense when the reference position failed to arrive at the appropriate time. My unfailing error was (a) being too keen and expecting things to happen too quickly and (b) being unaware that the place was coming up right under the nose of the plane and, therefore, hidden from view. In the latter case, the pin-point positioning had nothing to do with good navigation – just first-class luck. Arriving spot-on is the last thing you believe will happen, so you're forever looking to left and right, rather than over the front; and you end up buzzing right over it.

The final exercise in this department is the qualifying cross-country solo flight – the one you do before sending off the application forms for your PPL. It's compulsory, it's inevitable, it's the one which determines beyond any shadow of doubt whether or not you can be allowed into the skies on a permanent solo basis. More precisely, it's a three-landing trip to two distant airfields – one of which must be at least fifty miles from the starting field.

When you arrive, the managers or controllers of both alien fields should be sought out and asked to sign a special form – just to prove you've been there and haven't been swanning around in circles ten minutes up the road from home. These people should be treated with due respect, since the form asks them to comment on your join, circuit, approach and landing techniques. Be ever so humble, is my advice. I've never tried it myself, but you could try offering a magnum of Moët for their trouble.

Just for a change, my own qualifying cross-country went off rather well. The route was Edinburgh to Carlisle; Carlisle to Glenrothes – with a ten-minute sea trip across the mouth of the Firth of Forth; and Glenrothes back to Edinburgh. Both away landings were rated 'good' by the respective airfield controllers; not much to write home about, but a darn sight better than the alternative. Remarkably, I received an 'excellent' for airmanship from the Glenrothes manager when, to be honest, I considered my performance no better than average. Which just goes to show that there are some truly decent people in aviation and that, as in every endeavour, luck plays a not-so-modest part in flying training.

Apart from the qualifier, only one cross-country sticks out in my mind – the very first. A short hop of a mere seventy-five minutes, a flea-bite in the aviation scheme of things, and only two places to find: a middle-sized town called Kelso and a projection of land called St Abb's Head. But everything, and I mean everything, went wrong. In the first place, it was the day of a big rugby international: Scotland v France. There were more aircraft arriving at and departing from Edinburgh than you could shake a stick at. From private jets to 747s, from pusher monoplanes to Pitt's Specials. They were coming and going like starlings.

Was I worried? You can bank on it; and things began going awry the minute I climbed aboard uniform-fox.

To start with, Jock had to remind me from the apron, and in dumb show, to call ATC before taxi-ing. This I did, not only breaking in half way through a message directed at ATC from someone else but also acknowledging ATC's reply to that someone else. They put me right in short order. Next I was asked to give way to an RAF twin-engined Heron which was taxi-ing towards me. I did as I was bid but ham-fistedly left one wing-tip overhanging the taxiway. Now, the Heron could not fail to hit uniform-fox unless it stopped dead – so it did exactly that. In my turn, and with much throttle, brake and red face, I inched the 150 out of its path. Whatever must they have thought of me in that plane and also up in the tower? I didn't ask, but I imagined a lot of tutting and head-shaking going on.

The next ricket occurred ten miles out, when I told ATC approach that I was leaving the Control Zone at Penicuik, south-east of Edinburgh.

'What's your return time, uniform-fox?' they asked, nicely enough. Well, this wasn't the tower controller I'd had a few minutes back, so he wasn't *au fait* with the incompetent in uniform-fox. Yet.

I looked at my watch, it was 12.30 p.m. Quick as a flash, I added sixty-five minutes to it (I'd been flying for ten) and said: 'Estimate return time thirteen-thirty-five.'

'Is that thirteen-thirty-five zulu?'

'Eh?'

'Zulu,' he said. 'GMT.'

'Come again.'

'*Greenwich Mean Time.*' He was beginning to lose his cool.

I did some fast thinking. We were in the middle of April. Had the clocks gone backward, or forward? If so, was it now GMT or BST? My chances were two-to-one, so I took a stab.

'Affirmative,' I offered, 'zulu.'

He wasn't convinced. His voice came back over the air – now very tiredly. 'What is the duration of your flight, uniform-fox?'

'Sixty-five minutes.'

'In which case,' he replied, 'your return time is twelve-thirty-five, zulu.'

'Affirmative.' It was the only response I could make.

When this incident took place, about three years ago, zulu (GMT) was the recognized international standard time, but I happened to be operating on local time (BST). Hence, the discrepancy. However, GMT has now been replaced by UTC (Universal Co-ordinated Time – the initials don't match the words on account of the fact that our French cousins, who appear to be largely responsible for the change, tend to speak back to front). Anyway, UTC is now the time to quote when flying – that's assuming you can remember which way the clocks went at the last alteration.

I mention all of this at length only to show how a lack of knowledge – albeit a modest lack – can turn your entire world completely upside down. So nothing should be considered too nit-picky for you to bother about, because as sure as God made enquiring minds some bright spark will pose the question – and expect an answer.

But that little episode was mild compared with the problems yet to come.

Thirty-odd minutes' flying brought me within anxiety distance of the first pin-point – the town. As usual, I failed to spot it at first because, as usual, it was hidden beneath the engine cowling. Only a lucky backward glance located it fast disappearing under the tail, and I celebrated the find by doing a number of tight turns overhead oblivious Kelso.

The next target lay to the north-east according to the map, necessitating a course change of some 80°. I scrutinized my knee-pad (which, incidentally, I'd knocked up out of an old plastic clipboard and a length of velcrome-coated elastic) and read off the previously prepared new heading for St Abb's.

Before turning onto the new course, I checked the direction indicator against the compass. They should have read identically. Needless to say, they didn't – either the DI or the compass had wandered and I couldn't work out which. I figured it out eventually and reset the DI. But I'd been performing tight turns, had I not? The compass had not yet settled into equilibrium, with the result that, when I checked the DI again seconds later, it was still wrong and the felony was being compounded by the minute.

Now totally confused, I decided to fly straight and level – in no particular direction – to allow the instruments to compose themselves. This I did, but at the very moment I began re-re-readjusting the DI, on came ATC.

'Golf-uniform-foxtrot. What is your position and height?'

I snatched up the mike, shooting glances this way and that in an attempt to re-locate Kelso. Would you believe it wasn't there? It crossed my mind that I might give him the old position and height joke: 'I'm in the cockpit and five-feet-seven', but that might have brought more trouble than I was already in. So, even though I hadn't a clue where I was, I resolved to brazen it out.

'Edinburgh approach. This is golf-uniform-foxtrot. Leaving Kelso *en route* for St Abb's.'

Silence, then: 'Golf-uniform-foxtrot. What is your position and height?'

'Lost!' I said to myself, but repeated the '*en route* St Abb's' lie to ATC.

Again there was a pause, followed by a slow and deliberate

enunciation of: 'Golf-uniform-foxtrot. What is your position and height?'

This routine continued for three more choruses, with ATC doing the melody and me performing the descant.

Finally, someone tumbled that my radio was not functioning – I think it was me. No radio, I just could not believe my luck. I felt just as Colonel Custer must have felt when the Red Indian team turned up at the Little Big Horn ground for the all-American play-off. Sunk!

ATC came back.

'We have you on carrier-wave,' they told me calmly. Which meant that they could hear the mike button being pressed on frequency but were getting no voice. 'We believe you're receiving this transmission. Adopt carrier-wave code – press once for no, twice for yes.

I pressed twice, and as I did so, I fiddled with the radio's volume control and jiggled the on/off switch. All the time, I chatted away nervously and loudly. At one point I gave out with: 'Is there anybody down there wants to talk to anybody up here?!' Help from anywhere, even the spirit world, would have been received with grateful thanks.

As you've guessed, ATC picked up that last offering. 'Ah, you're back with us,' a kindly voice said; and I could hear the smile in the voice.

From then on, there was no more trouble with the radio. Subsequent tests failed to reveal any fault, and my conclusion is that I had very likely put the mockers on it some way, somehow. Never mind Yuri Geller, I've forever had this adverse influence on machinery. As my dear wife often comments: 'You've got a face such as would stop a clock!' Nobody else, afterwards, experienced the radio problem, I'm pleased to say. So it must have been me and my psychokinetic face.

With that bit of excitement under my belt, I arrived at St Abb's incidentless. 'Arrived' isn't quite the right word, since I hit the coast half-a-dozen miles downstream of it near Coldingham. But it was a real treat motoring up the North Sea, my first experience of trans-oceanic travel solo.

The penultimate farce of the day was brought off after re-entering the zone and preparing for landing. I was approached once again by ATC for my position and height, which I gave. They then threw a curly one at me. Report at Corstorphine Hill, they enjoined.

Between thee and me, I didn't know Corstorphine Hill from a hole in the wall. All right, it's a local reporting point and one I should have been familiar with. But if I have anything that even mildly resembles a strong subject, it certainly isn't geography. Indeed, I'm quite regularly confused about getting home from an office I've worked in for five years. Lack of observation is the problem, and laziness the cause. What earthly good, I've always maintained, is the knowledge that Acacia Avenue meets Sebastapol Terrace at Chinese Restaurant corner? Moreover, I would be agog with indifference when listening to people describing a journey, say, from Neasden to Thornton Heath (or Fort Neef, as Londoners are wont to call it) with every bollard, pedestrian crossing and traffic light thrown in. Well, it always seemed a maddening waste of time having to stand there pretending to absorb each detailed trifle. Frankly, I'd rather have watched porridge set.

It's different now, of course; and I can spend a good twenty minutes – more if uninterrupted – on such subjects as Newcastle city centre roadworks and the Glasgow one-way system. I learned my lesson – with bells on.

If you've never been fortunate enough to visit Edinburgh, let me tell you that the entire conurbation is surrounded by hills. Corstorphine Hill, therefore, was going to take some weeding out. My map showed the suburb clear enough, but no hill. Once again, I made up my mind to flannel through. A place resembling Corstorphine was close at hand; it could have been anywhere . . . and it was.

I reported, anyway. 'This is golf-uniform-foxtrot overhead Corstorphine Hill.'

I could almost hear them bursting their sides in the tower. 'Roger, uniform-fox. We have you in sight. You will arrive Corstorphine in two minutes, if you maintain present heading. *Report Corstorphine Hill*.'

Which was saying, in other words, that as a navigator I'd make a pretty good embalmer's mate. All I wanted to do at this stage was hit the deck and repair to the bar. Every drop of jack-the-lad had long since evaporated; and any resemblance I may have had to Coco the Clown was purely authentic.

ATC did a grand job, nevertheless, moving other aircraft out of my path and generally preparing themselves for the Last Coming. Despite their best efforts, however, I was about to execute the blunderous *dénouement*. So eager was I to get onto the runway after a morning playing charades that in lowering the flaps I hit the lever with a knuckle and inadvertently raised them again. It was to be a no-flap landing, my first, and I was oblivious to what wonders I was about to perform.

The initial impression was that uniform-fox appeared to be moving a little faster on the approach than usual, even though I'd throttled right back. I brought her nose up to decay the speed, but she continued to plough on. Over the threshold at fifteen feet and the ASI was up in the 80 mphs when it should have been in the sixties. What was wrong? It was a question I'd been posing for most of the morning. What more *was* there to go wrong?

I made a fast check around the instrument panel and finally noticed the flap lever. Should I leave it or apply some? I dithered between yes and no for long seconds, all the while skating along just feet above the runway. I eventually decided on 'no'. Good thing, really. I'm told that one or two quite spectacular things would have happened had I lowered flap at that speed and attitude. In the first place, the nose would have risen. Second, flying speed would have decayed rapidly, dropping the aircraft onto the concrete, possibly collapsing the undercarriage. Third, uniform-fox, student pilot and all would have spent some considerable time at the menders!

She floated for about a fortnight after I rounded out. The credits of my past life started to roll to the accompaniment of a single, shouted, long-drawn-out word: a four-letter one not dissimilar from that used by Redford and Newman when leaping from that cliff in the Butch Cassidy film.

Was I committed or wasn't I? Should I open up and go round again? The problem resolved itself in short order, in one of the gentlest landings in which I've ever taken part. Uniform-fox did the ladylike thing: she lowered her legs discreetly, placing her neat little feet elegantly upon the ground.

What lessons are to be learned from this series of discomfitures? Quite a few.

LESSONS LEARNED

Your instructor can teach you only so much in the time allowed him. He positively does expect you to undertake a bit of homework, such as reading the appropriate volumes and making yourself acquainted with matters UTC and BST; getting to grips, in the privacy of your own home, with a map or two in order to discover the lie of at least the local land; and knowing what action to take when your radio goes duff. In my case, I should and would have diverted to a smaller airfield had the radio proved completely unserviceable. The risk involved in returning to Edinburgh, with half the French civil airfleet on site, would have been too great even for me to contemplate.

What's more, your instructor cannot be blamed when you fail to discharge such simple tasks as aligning DI with compass. He will have talked himself hoarse on this and other themes, and you will have nodded in apparent understanding. Chances are, though, you'll long-finger coming to immediate terms with these bits of knowledge, believing that practical use of same is months away and you'll get round to knowing them in good time. In reality, however, it isn't and you probably won't.

During this period of training, you'll be working flat out to qualify for your final handling test – the test which once and for all establishes your competence in every aspect of airmanship. The test is monitored by a qualified CAA examiner who, if you are lucky, could well be your instructor. Not that you won't have to pull out all the stops no matter who examines you. Final handling tests last for about an hour – sixty minutes' worth of distance well and truly run.

While you're enduring the trials and tribulations of clocking up hours – making unnecessary mistakes with a frightening regularity – you may care to find solace in the words of a senior air-traffic controller of my acquaintance who maintains: 'The minute anyone steps into an aircraft, they leave fifty per cent of their brains on the ground.'

How very true.

SUMMARY

The Principles of Instrument Flying

(a) When flying on instruments in cloud, with no horizon to refer to, and thus almost totally blind, the pilot must ignore his own sense of equilibrium. It is quite possible, in these conditions, to be flying upside down without realizing it.

There is a story (probably apocryphal – but it illustrates the point) that two aircraft going in opposite directions passed at close quarters. Each appeared to the other to be totally inverted, but which of them was the right way up?

(b) Learn to rely implicitly on what the flight instruments tell you.

(c) Make all your turns rate-one turns, i.e. no more than 16° of bank.

(d) When turning onto a new heading (new course), bank left for the 'low' numbers and right for the 'high' ones. In other words, when turning from say, 090° onto 010°, turn left; when turning from 270° to 360°, turn right.

The Air Traffic Control Service is an Advisory Service Only

(i) For all kinds of legal reasons, ATC does not issue hard-and-fast commands. In effect, the ATC service merely monitors what is happening in the air and 'advises' pilots on what actions to take.

(ii) ATC will not, then, willingly involve themselves in hazardous situations to a point at which they might ultimately become responsible for the outcome. To put it another way: the pilot has the final responsibility for the safety of his passengers, himself and his aircraft at all times. Correct course-keeping and the maintenance of safe separation from other aircraft are his responsibility wholly and solely. And this applies even when he is being 'controlled' by ATC.

(iii) However, anyone who ignores or deliberately acts against an ATC directive is asking for trouble. Clearly, the tower has a complete picture of what's going on, while the pilot is aware only of events in his immediate sphere of operations. Not only that: offenders against ATC soon feel the full weight of the Civil Aviation Authority on their necks.

(iv) Notwithstanding the above, when asked for assistance, ATC will move with some alacrity. To get their full and undivided attention in a tricky situation (you are uncertain of your position or have inadvertently run into a bank of cloud from which there appears no likely exit), all you have to do is relay the circumstances and request their help. This takes the onus off them and they are able to advise you accordingly.

In the event that you go on to declare an emergency, ATC will move heaven and earth to get you safely back on the ground.

But *you* must make the first move.

Radar Surveillance

It is a fallacy to suppose that, wherever you fly in the United Kingdom, you will be given radar surveillance as a matter of course. You won't.

While most major civil airfields and all military airfields keep a regular radar watch, the civil types do so only during their operating hours and as a kind of tool for the safe management of the airfield and its surrounding air-traffic zone. Which means that the purpose of radar is not to help get pilots out of trouble, although it very frequently is recruited to this end. Rather, it is a traffic co-ordinator. To put it plainly: a pilot should never expect to be monitored on radar; when he is, he may consider it a bonus.

(i) I have found, particularly at Edinburgh airport, that ATC are only too happy to take part in exercises involving radar – radar-assisted approaches, for instance, where the pilot's position is first located on the scope and where he is subsequently given headings to steer until he arrives within sight (makes visual contact) of the airfield.

These exercises are first-class experience for the pilot and the controller – especially if either or both are trainees.

Navigation

Apart from the actual handling of an aircraft, navigation is perhaps the single most important element in flying training. It therefore pays to give this subject the attention it deserves.

During your flying training, you will be given cross-country exercises to perform – these will be accomplished either dual or solo. Either way, you must have a course to fly; and this course will be better off for having been conceived and noted down while you are still on the ground.

Yes, a course can be worked out in the air – and often will be, since wind changes or unforeseen diversions to other destinations make this sometimes necessary. Yes, you can take the paraphernalia of maps, navigation computer and calculator into the air with you (and you'd be foolish not to), but how much easier to initiate a flight-log which has details of your course, estimated airspeed/groundspeed, estimated time of arrival etc all worked out before you go.

This way, you simply set the course, carry your map on your lap – the easier to check landmarks as they appear – and fly unencumbered and relaxed. The correct completion of a flight-log comes as part of your training; and once you've got into the habit, it will come as second nature.

8 Weather Lore and Weather Sense

Once you start flying training, you'll find yourself taking a more than passing interest in the weather. That interest will be even greater once you qualify, because then you'll have no instructor to refer to for a yea or nay on a proposed flight. Weather is the critical factor in our kind of aviation, and you must resign yourself at a very early stage to playing second fiddle to it – to being rained off, snowed in and fog-bound, with flying postponed for the duration. It's frustrating – extremely so, yet there's nothing to be done about it unless you're a dab hand at parting seas and driving back waves.

As the man said: 'When it rains, I let it.'

Maybe the day will arrive when science is advanced enough to give us full control of the weather, though I strongly doubt it. Just think how dreadfully dull (or dreadfully sunny, perhaps, depending on whose turn it is to get the good stuff) that situation could prove to be. For the times I've arrived at the field for a detail only to be told it's off due to poor visibility, when a mile or two away the air is champagne clear, are countless; but the subsequent tirade against the elements helped no end in exorcizing the emotions of a rotten working week.

What is remarkable about the weather, insofar as we are concerned, is just how quickly it changes. A vicious wind, capable of overturning a taxi-ing plane, can develop out of a breeze which five minutes before wouldn't have rippled grass; and a blinding fog can creep in, as I hope to demonstrate, straight out of a clear blue sky. Both events are anathema to the airman and should be taken into permanent account. Good enough reason, certainly, to have a working knowledge of the whys and wherefores of the weather, plus an inkling of what's likely to happen in a given set of circumstances. Then, at least, you can take an educated guess about whether to continue a flight or abort; to estimate the most favourable route around a hailstorm; and generally to predict the imminence of any of those conditions that heaven is thinking of chucking at you.

Nobody but a fool goes anywhere in the light of an adverse Met report. Nevertheless, given that weather forecasting isn't a particularly exact science, you can be caught flat-footed relying too implicitly on an official forecast when, if you know even a little bit about it, you might conclude something completely different from what you've been told.

A current Met report, combined with personal judgement based on prevailing local conditions, is the only way to fly.

HOW CLOUDS FORM

The greater part of your flying career will be spent at close range to cloud. We therefore begin this section by observing some clouds.

We should understand a thing or two about the way clouds are formed before we look at cloud formation in a physical sense. You'll doubtless know it already, but just in case you've forgotten . . .

The air around us contains water vapour in varying quantities, and the precise amount is measurable in terms of humidity. Additionally, the make-up of air in various parts of the world contains more or less water depending on location. Consequently these differing air masses have differing humidities. The masses are categorized as Maritime and Continental – both of which are subdivided as polar and tropical. They speak for themselves.

When a high-humidity air mass rises, its temperature drops, and as it gets to the point where further cooling would cause condensation, it is said to have reached its dew-point. Incidentally, the air temperature change with altitude is known as the Lapse Rate and calculates out at 2°C per thousand feet.

Who needs it? you ask. You do, I reply. You will invariably find a question or three on dew-point and related themes in the Met paper. That being the case, you might think it well worth while burning some midnight oil over a meteorology textbook. Anyway, I had to – why shouldn't you?

Clouds are formed, therefore, when air containing water vapour rises, expands and cools adiabetically. (Better read up 'adiabetic', too. It comes wet and dry, like emery paper, but is far too involved to go into here.) The cloud can be in the form of water droplets, ice crystals or a mixture of both. Moreover, the type of cloud that's formed is largely dependent upon the height at which the air mass condenses out.

CLOUD FORMATIONS

Now for cloud formations. There are four types. Once more, we bring an acronym into play:

CASH, standing for: Cirrus, Alto, Stratus, Heaped (Cumulus). Strictly speaking, there is no such cloud as Alto, the word being the prefix to the variants in that category – but it's easy to remember. Each of the four main types also has a number of sub-orders.

	CIRRUS (Ci)	*High*
	Has diverging filaments, not unlike	From
	hair or wool, that are distinct from	16,500
	one another.	to
C.	*CIRROCUMULUS* (Cc)	45,000
	The traditional mackerel sky.	feet
	CIRROSTRATUS (Cs)	
	A thin white cloud patch with	
	veil-like appearance.	
	ALTOCUMULUS (Ac)	*Medium*
	Like sea-rippled sand at low	From
	tide.	6,500
A.	*ALTOSTRATUS* (As)	to
	Often gives a translucent	23,000
	appearance to the sun.	feet
	STRATUS (St)	
	Low-lying dark grey cloud –	

S.	dirty in appearance. *NIMBOSTRATUS* (Ns) Thick rain cloud, becoming ragged over high ground. *STRATOCUMULUS* (Sc) Light grey rolls with dark patches.	*Low* From zero to 6,500 feet
H.	*CUMULUS* (Cu) Fluffy clouds like puffs of smoke with flattened bottoms. *CUMULONIMBUS* (Cb) The thunderhead. A dense, heavy cloud of considerable vertical extent and often with an anvil top.	*Heaped* From 1,000 to 40,000 feet, ranging throughout the cloud spectrum.

Note: The letters in brackets after each type represent the abbreviation used by Met offices.

That's the bones of it, although there are quite a few variations on each cloud theme. Luckily, we've no need to go any farther for the purposes of a PPL. Fig. 16 should give a clearer idea of where various clouds turn up in the aerial scheme of things.

Cumulonimbus ('cunims' for short) are the kinds of clouds to be given a very wide berth. They are chaos personified. At best, they contain rain and turbulence. At worst, they are running alive with hail, ice and electrical activity. The up-currents and downdraughts in some cunims will render a plane uncontrollable and cause severe structural damage – even rip the wings out by the roots. Experts advise flyers to stay well clear of cunims, but where an encounter is unavoidable, the finest course of action is to use the barest minimum of stick and rudder, so as to take as much pressure as possible off control surfaces. This procedure should also be practised when flying through any kind of turbulence – don't over-correct: it gets you nothing but baleful stares from sea-green passengers.

Hailstones can also be something of a problem, unnerving more than anything else, though hail has been recorded the size of golfballs and that's certainly no laughing matter. A few

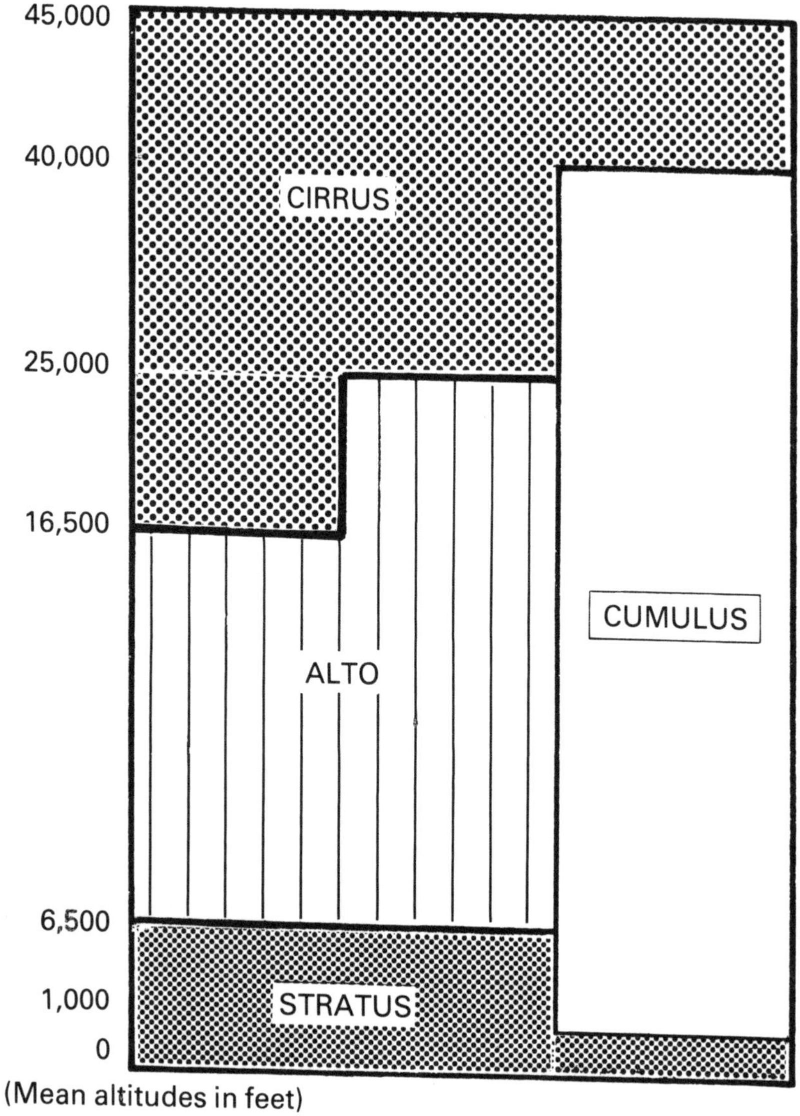
45,000
40,000
25,000
16,500
6,500
1,000
0
CIRRUS
ALTO
CUMULUS
STRATUS
(Mean altitudes in feet)

of those clattering onto fuselage and wings would capture your attention pretty rapidly, I should think.

LIGHTNING, ICE AND FOG

Lightning? There are plenty of myths surrounding it and lots of well-embroidered stories recording its horrors, but aircraft are built to take it. A lightning strike, I'm reliably informed, diffuses throughout the airframe via a bonding of parts in electrical continuity. That doesn't mean to say it won't play all hell with the flight instruments and have everyone aboard composing their own private arrangements with their Maker.

Icing, on the other hand, is a very real hazard and one that must be watched for, even in conditions where logically it shouldn't occur. There are several kinds of ice, and several parts of the airframe it will affect.

There's hoar frost, the stuff that's a pest on car windscreens, usually picked up overnight by aircraft parked in the open but also encounterable when descending from cool altitudes to warmer ones. There's rime ice, which looks like icing sugar and builds up on flying surfaces while in flight. This one, unlike the next, will disappear quickly when warmer climes are headed for.

The real killer is glazed or clear ice. It's caused when super-cooled water particles collide with the leading edge of a wing – they impact, stick and freeze – growing in mass as more drops collect. The result is an irregular accumulation the length of the wing, disfiguring the aerofoil, extirpating the airflow and endowing the wing with all the lift characteristics of a manhole cover!

The other type of icing, as I've already mentioned, is carburettor icing. You are made aware of its presence by a gradual drop in engine revs . . . and sometimes you aren't. The answer is to apply carb heat for a few seconds on a regular basis, even when you know the air temperature is above freezing. In fact, use it *particularly* when you know there's no

---

Fig. 16. Cloud Types. There are four types of cloud. Each has a quite distinctive appearance, and each can be found at more or less determinate altitudes

danger of icing. That way you get into a worthwhile habit, and you keep your engine doing what it should be doing if you've guessed wrongly. Running.

What about fog? Well, here's a little beauty that flyers just love to hate. They never tire of telling you so, either. Happily, with a touch of nous and forethought, fog is predictable – radiation fog, that is. Here's how.

Take one large mass of moist air. Mix together with a *soupçon* of temperature inversion and cover with a nice clear sky. In other words, the ingredients for radiation fog are: (a) a clear sky; (b) a warm air-mass whose lower surface cools rapidly on contact with a cold ground surface – that's the temperature inversion; (c) an easily reached dew-point for condensing out in the form of fog, and (d) a light breeze to blend everything together.

So look for a warm spell following coldish weather, and fog could well be imminent. As you will realize, a clouded sky will prevent heat loss from the surface; therefore the sky must be clear for radiation fog to form. So much for the line: 'On a clear day, you can see forever.' Not always true.

There are, for the record, other types of fog: advection fog, hill fog and sea fog – to name but a few. As a rule, you need plenty of cloud around for these to form, so they're not as important from the PPL's point of view, bearing in mind that he shouldn't be messing around in cloud anyway.

Lastly, rain, no big deal for the aviator (the same applies to sleet and snow, though visibility will be impaired to a greater extent with the latter). And no big deal even in aircraft without windscreen-wipers, which means all but the most sophisticated of single-engine planes. A propeller, you see, does a thorough job of clearing precipitation from windscreens via the blast created by slipstream.

Rain comes about, as you doubtless know, when water-vapour particles in cloud conjoin and become large enough to overcome both gravity and updraughts.

REGIONAL PRESSURE DIFFERENCES

There is much more than given above to be learned about meteorology before reaching PPL standard. A grasp of frontal systems, for instance, depressions, anticyclones and such is required of the student – arguably all far too involved to go into here. Of more practical use at the moment is a better understanding of regional pressure changes and how they affect altimeter settings.

In Chapter 3 we spoke about QFE and QNH – QFE being the setting which reads ground zero at a given airfield, irrespective of that airfield's height above sea-level, while QNH is one of two possible measurements: either the setting for an airfield's control zone or, once out of the zone, the setting for a region – of which there are fourteen in the British Isles. QNH gives the minimum pressure value for the area, and thus the pilot's altitude above sea-level. With it, he can determine with some accuracy the height at which to fly so as to avoid natural and man-made obstacles in that region.

The picture alters when he moves from one region to another, due to the pressure changes. Indeed, there can be quite marked pressure differences within the same region.

Consider, if you will, Mr Buys Ballot's Law. He states that, if you stand with your back to the wind anywhere in the northern hemisphere, the area of low pressure is to your left. That axiom quite clearly proves that winds move clockwise around a high-pressure system (veering) and anticlockwise

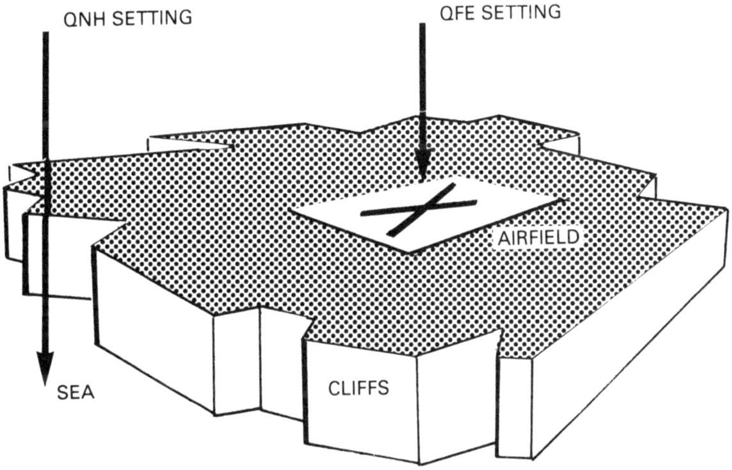

Fig. 17. The difference between QNH and QFE

around a low-pressure system (backing). Given this to be true and imagining we are flying along with a wind coming in from our left, we can expect to be moving into a low-pressure area.

Assume, too, that we are unable to request an updated QNH by radio from the local information service. What exactly are we getting into? Well, it's not unreasonable to suppose that, because we're moving towards a low-pressure area from a high-pressure area, our previously set QNH will become steadily more inaccurate. Essentially, if pressure drops, the altimeter over-reads.

This means that, in maintaining a given height with a high-pressure setting, we are in fact losing height as we move into the low-pressure area. In the example given here, the difference between the high and the low is 10 millibars. At 30 feet per millibar, the more important difference is 300 feet.

To save a great deal of messing about, especially for the airline boys and, indeed, light aircraft when we're lucky enough to be able to fly at decent altitudes, there is a thing called an International Standard Atmosphere, of which the component parts are: temperature 15°C; pressure 1013.2 millibars (or 29.92 inches of mercury); weight 14.7 lbs psi This standard comes into play at what's known as 'transition level', whereafter all references to height are given as 'flight levels'. In the UK transition level is 3,000 feet. At and above

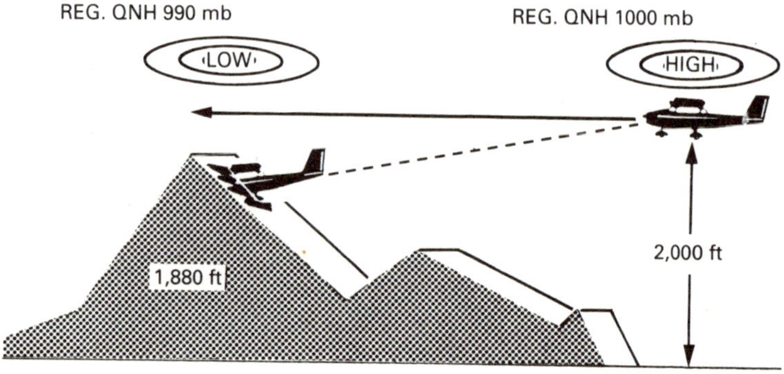

Fig. 18. The difference between the high and the low pressure is 10 millibars. 10 × 30 = 300 feet. If we maintain 2,000 feet by our original altimeter setting, we'll hit the hill 180 feet from the summit

that level, everybody adopts the same altimeter setting of 1013.2 mbs. It's all very logical, in that the separation of aircraft is carried out to a common and fixed denominator.

Here endeth more or less everything I know about meteorology.

SUMMARY

Ice Can Be a Killer

Ice that can be seen, when it's glistening on wings on a sunny winter's morning, can be dealt with. But it becomes deadly when it invades a carburettor or when it begins to build up on leading edges of wings during flight. Apart from that, ice can play havoc with instruments if it becomes heavy enough to block a pitot tube.

Which is one good reason why pitot tubes are universally fitted with their own heater.

BEFORE MAKING ANY TRIP, ALWAYS TAKE THE TROUBLE TO PICK UP A MET REPORT.

If an Altimeter is Incorrectly Set, the Pilot is Asking for Trouble

Regional QNH or airfield QFE should be set on your altimeter the minute you receive it. The difference could mean several hundred feet on the clock – the difference between flying over a hill and trying to fly through it!

The Ingredients of the International Standard Atmosphere

(a) Temperature: 15°C.
(b) Pressure: 1013.2 millibars.
(c) Weight (gravity): 14.7 lbs per square inch

9 Air Law – The Bare Essentials

With an ordinary, everyday PPL, there's only one way you can fly. That's under Visual Flight Rules. The rules insist that you be:

(a) One nautical mile horizontally, and 1,000 feet vertically distanced from cloud – with a flight visibility of five nautical miles.

(b) And when operating outside controlled airspace at altitudes below 3,000 feet (above sea-level), you must be within sight of the surface and clear of cloud.

These rules can only be carried out under what is known as Visual Meteorological Conditions to what are also known as Visual Flight Rules; and unless you are given a *special* VFR clearance by ATC – which temporarily lowers the visual threshold somewhat – the rules must be obeyed to the letter. The emphasis, here, is on flying with visual contact with the ground. Under no circumstances must a PPL deliberately lose this contact. It follows, therefore, that a PPL may not fly in cloud or at night. You can, however, obtain further qualifications which allow you to fly in less favourable conditions. You can pick up a Night Rating in just a few hours, and a little determined effort will bring an Instrument Meteorological Conditions rating. Both will widen your horizons, so to speak; and a full Instrument Rating will allow you to 'go airways' and fly upstairs with the Tridents and Jumbos. Always supposing you have the need and the nerve.

We've spoken about controlled airspace; let's clarify it. The area around an airfield, from ground-level to a specified height, in which aircraft must conform to ATC rules is a Control Zone. A Control Area is a wadge of airspace controlled from a given height above ground to another given height. Joining both of these are airways, corridors that link heavy traffic centres to each other.

You'll discover that there are dozens more places where only the foolhardy or the well-qualified venture, such as military airfield traffic zones, AIAAs – areas of intense aerial activity, and suchlike forbidden and forbidding places. Not that the RAF will shoot you down if you accidentally wander into their stamping grounds. Even so, you might receive the all-time surprise of your life if you happen to get mixed up with a flight of 50+ Phantoms doing a formation exercise.

AIRFIELD GROUND SIGNALS

You might confidently expect, in these days of automatic landing devices, radar, micro this and that, and computer something else, that electronics would be the sole communications medium. You might even be forgiven for expecting that such old-fashioned devices as ground signals, flags, flares and flashlamps for correspondence between ground and air would have been decently interred with their Victorian inventors. Don't you believe it. Many, many airfields still aren't yet equipped with radio, never mind radar. And even on fields where radio is installed, what happens if said transmitter goes on the blink or if incoming flights have no radio themselves? Precisely, you resort to visual communication.

The illustration shows the kind of ground signals to watch for in the above circumstances. Usually, there's an area set aside on the field specifically for their display.

Light signals are also used and these can be made with lamps or pyrotechnically with flares.

Signal	*To aircraft in flight*	*To aircraft on the ground*
Intermittent green light.	Return to airfield circuit – await landing permission.	Authorizes aircraft to taxi.
Continuous green light.	You may land.	You may take off.
Intermittent red light.	Runway unfit – land elsewhere.	Move/clear of landing strip immediately.

GROUND SIGNALS

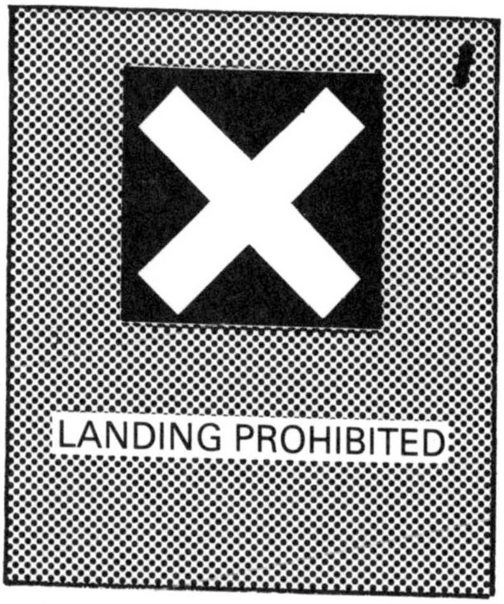

Landing prohibited
A red square panel with yellow strips across each diagonal. Unsafe – landing forbidden.

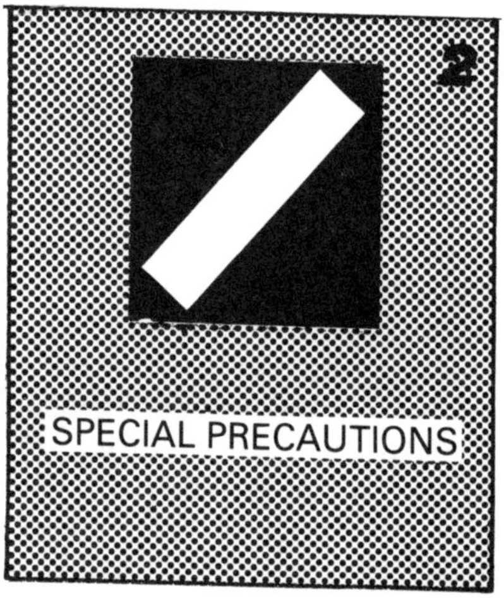

Special precautions
A red square panel with one yellow diagonal. Take care – obstruction

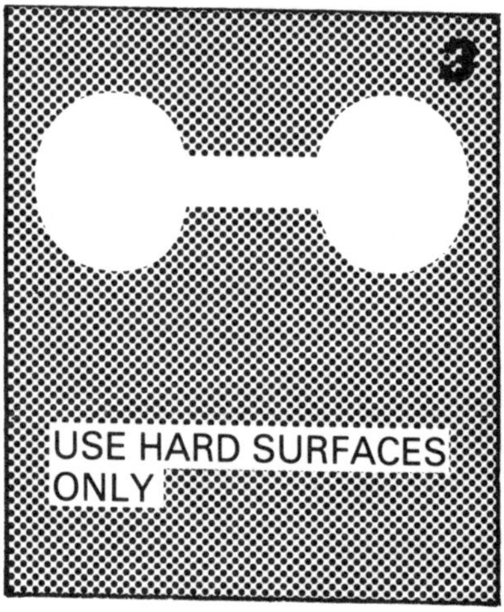

Use hard surfaces only
White dumb-bell. Ground movements confined to metalled surfaces only.

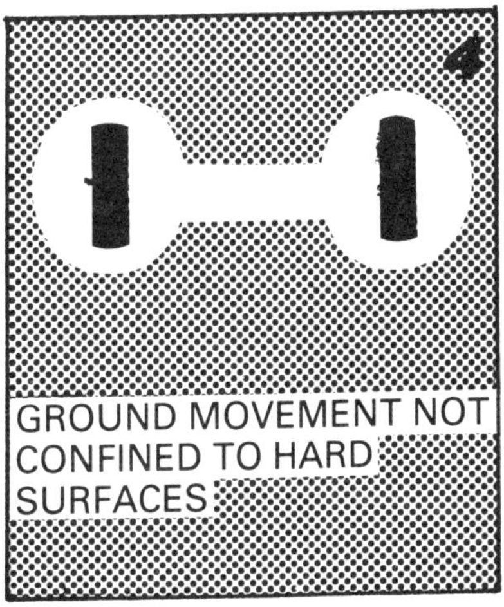

Hard and grass surfaces for movements
White dumb-bell with black bars. Land and take-off on hard surfaces only – but movement is not confined to runways.

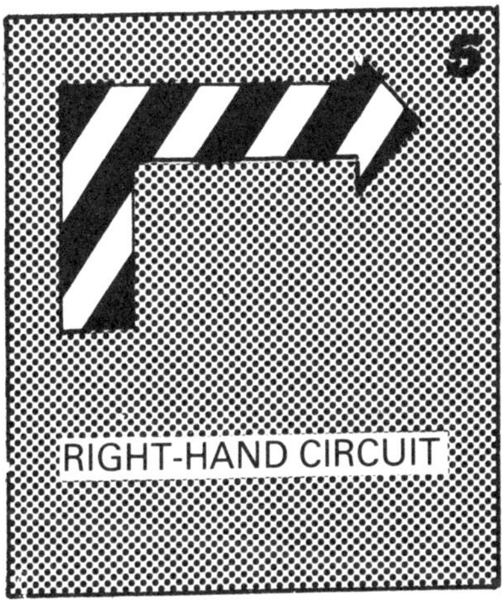

Right-hand circuits
A red-and-yellow striped arrow. Right-hand circuit operating.

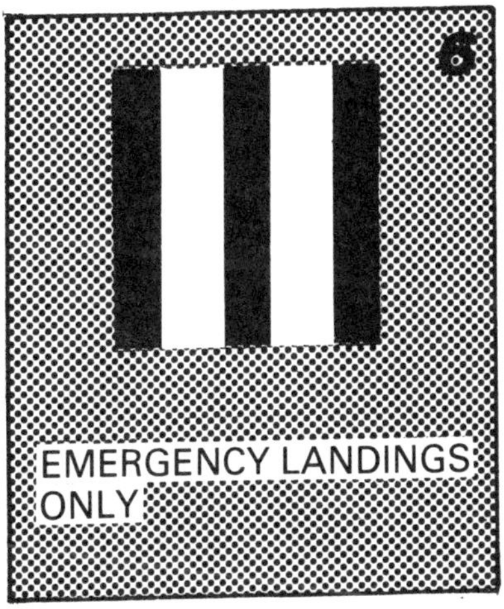

Emergency landings only
A red square with two vertical yellow bars. Aircraft landings in emergency only.

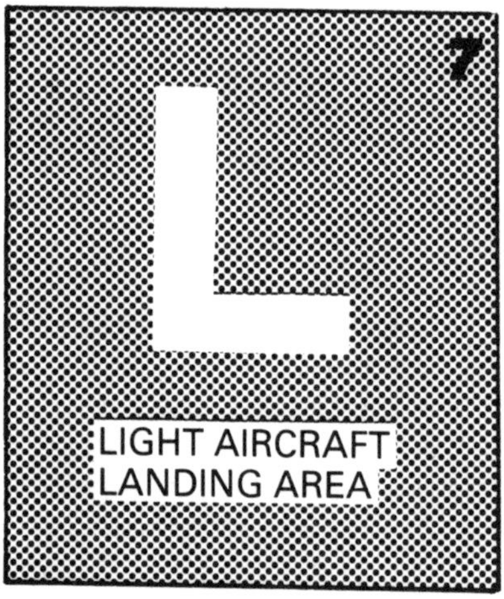

Light aircraft landing area
A white L shows the area for take-off and landing of light aircraft only.

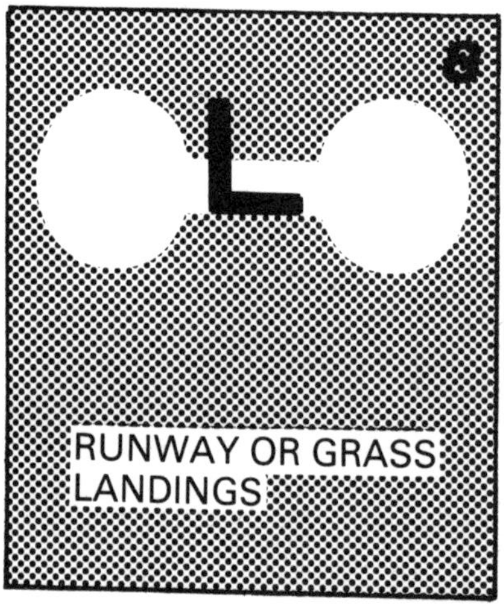

Land on runway or area designated by L
A red letter L on dumb-bell signifies that light aircraft may land on the runway or grass area designated in 7.

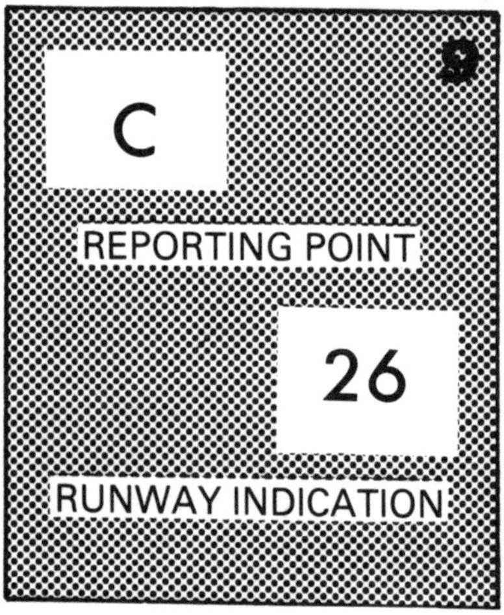

Above: **Reporting point**
Black letter C on yellow background shows position of ATC or airfield management.
Below: **Runway indication**
Black numerals on a yellow background indicate the runway in use.

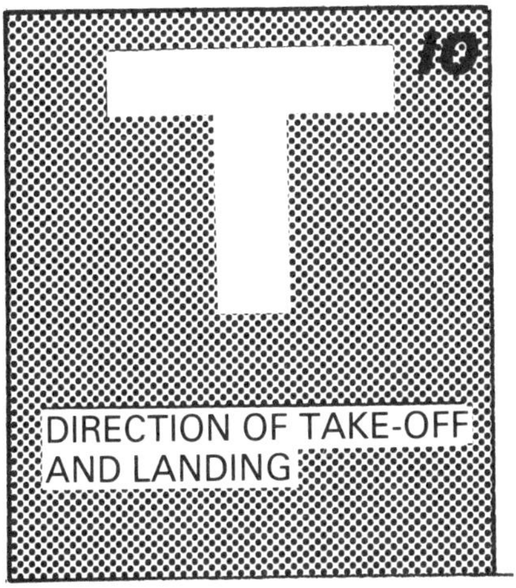

Direction of take-off and landing
A white T denotes that aircraft should take-off and land in the direction of the shaft.

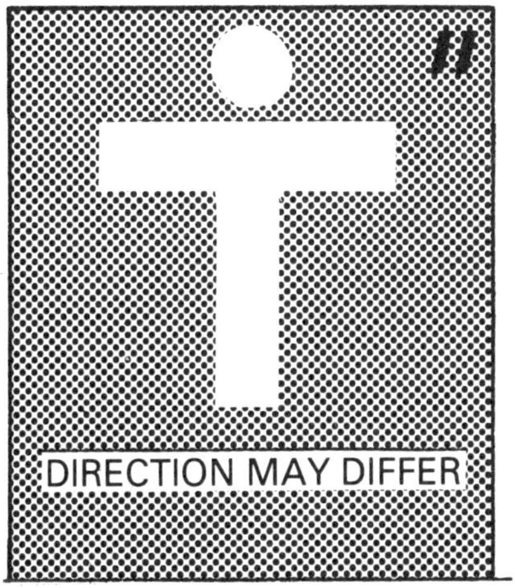

Direction of take-off and landing may differ
The same white T with a white disc signifies that the directions of landing and take-off may differ.

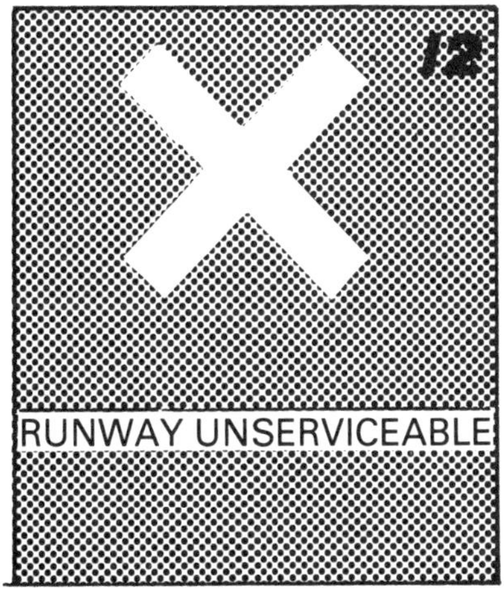

Runway unserviceable
A white cross at the threshold of a runway or taxiway denotes that the surface is unfit for use.

Fig. 19. Ground signals

Continuous red light.	Give way to other aircraft.	Stay where you are. Stop.
Intermittent white light.	Land after receiving continuous green.	Return to apron.
Red flare.	Wait for permission to land.	
Black or white smoke projectiles (day).	Alter heading – you are in a prohibited area.	
Bursting green stars.	You are in a prohibited area – land at nearest airfield.	

AIRCRAFT NAVIGATION LIGHTS

Aircraft are also required to carry navigation lights if they are approved for night flying. The three lights – red, green and white, each of five candella or more – are arranged in such a way that only one light can be viewed at any given time. (Except, that is, in a head-on situation.)

I'll explain the significance of that in a moment. In the meantime, the illustration shows how the lights are positioned. The starboard wing carries a green light and is visible through 110°. Similarly, the port wing is red at 110°. While the tail-light is white and shows through 140°. Now the reason why. Imagine flying at night and spotting a red light at the same altitude as yourself, but slightly to the right. You can assume, without the shadow of doubt, that the other fellow is crossing your path at something like an acute angle. You must then take the necessary avoiding action. Were you also able to see his white tail-light, you might assume that he is on more or less the same heading as yourself and not be too worried – which could be fatal. So the one-light-at-a-time system shows graphically the direction in which the other aircraft is travelling. To put it another way, should you spot a green light in similar circumstances, i.e. to your right, there would be no danger, because he has already gone past, left to right.

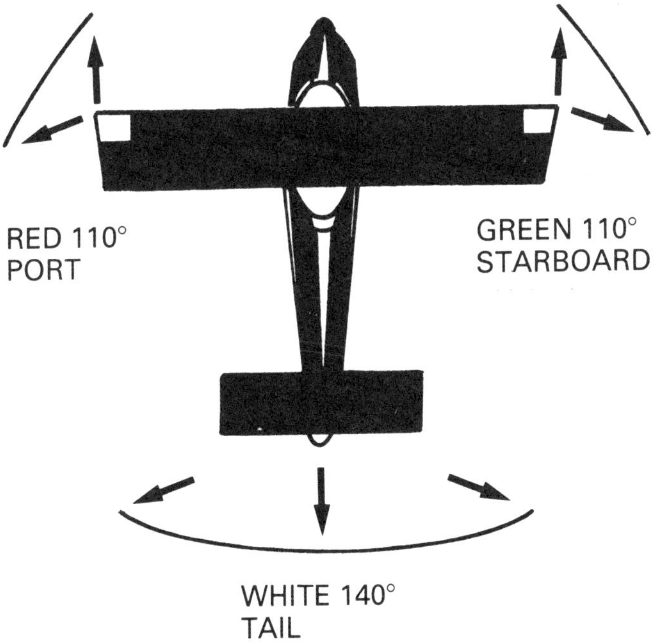

Fig. 20. Aircraft navigation lights

DRIVE ON THE RIGHT

The rule of the flying road is the same as with maritime practice: you drive on the right. This rule is observed on the ground as well as in the air. Where two aircraft are approaching head on, both must alter course to the right. In flight, the aircraft which has another on its right – as in converging courses from ahead and behind – the one which has the other on its right is duty-bound to give way. Again, where one plane is overtaking another on the same course, the faster plane must turn to starboard. The only exception is for an aircraft overtaking another on the ground: it alters direction to the left.

If you want to know more, or see more, on air law, there are plenty of good books on the subject. What you've got here, nevertheless, is enough to make you a proper smart alec at your first ground training evening class!

SUMMARY

1. Acquaint yourself with all the control zones in your area.
2. Get to know the areas of intense aerial activity in your region.
3. Find out the locations and heights of all man-made aerial obstructions – radio masts, beacons, chimneys – in your vicinity.
4. You will need to learn ground signal displays by heart for your air-law exam.
5. Good airmanship begins with a sound understanding of air law.
6. The CAA publications *Air Pilot* and *NOTAMS,* which your club should subscribe to, will keep you up to date on most of the above.

10 A Funny Thing Happened on the Way to the Holding Point . . .

This chapter is a collection of all the bits and pieces of information and anecdote that don't seem to fit anywhere else. (Leastways, I can't make them fit.) It's a compilation of those myriad questions that bugged my mind in the early days – questions that could only be asked *sotto voce* in quiet corners for fear of being laughed out of the club.

Let's put it this way. I came to flying wide-eyed and green from the waist up. I came with no previous experience, no maths, no geography, no discipline, and I brought all the innate indolence of my profession – indeed, it's an occupation that couldn't be more contraposed to the activity I hoped to pursue. Ten hours a day, all I do is recycle clichés. To be truthful, putting squiggles on bits of paper in a smoke-filled office, situated just two doors up from an all-day opening pub, is hardly the training ground for mental and physical efficiency or split-second decision-making.

Some nights I would attend evening class and be in tremendous awe of the other students, who appeared so much brighter and so much faster on the uptake than I. The majority would wade in and grasp the essence of a lecture while I was still trying to unfasten my briefcase.

Things have changed now, though. Because I applied myself. I can now open a briefcase pretty quickly. Undoubtedly, you are far better at copping onto things than I ever was. But just in case, here are a few points to ponder.

IN EMERGENCY, DIAL 121.5

Not too many hours had passed before it dawned on me that the machine I was flying was man-made and therefore subject to man's flaws. It could break down, catch fire or blow up any time it felt like it. Worse, after only an hour or two in the air, it struck me that Jock was the only one of the two of us who knew how to re-embrace *terra firma*. What would I do, therefore, if he suddenly had a fit of the vapours or decided, for whatever reason, to bale out? The answer, I now know, is to holler 'Emergency!'

There are two grades of emergency: Mayday and Pan.

Mayday is the big one, the one that has everybody on the ground hopping onto fire-engines, donning heat-masks or, for all I know, making a dash for the underground shelters. To call a Mayday, you really have to be in lots of trouble – serious trouble. Engine gone, fire in the cabin, that sort of thing.

The Emergency Service in the UK operates on a frequency of 121.5 MHz and keeps an around-the-clock vigil at that place on the dial. After finding the frequency, here's what you say: 'Mayday, Mayday, Mayday. This is golf-uniform-foxtrot. Cessna 150. Engine fire; repeat, engine fire. Request immediate landing at Edinburgh. Four miles east of Edinburgh at 3,000 feet.'

Your message will be acknowledged on the double, and you will be the most popular person in the country from then on – a superstar. All other aircraft movement in the area will be diverted, and you will have the full and undivided attention of the controller. All right, he's been sitting by that radio possibly for years, with nothing to occupy his mind but the *Daily Telegraph* crossword and his crochet-work, so he welcomes the distraction.

Pan is a little less fraught. You make this call, on the local tower frequency if possible, if and when a passenger is taken ill (mine invariably are but are far too polite to say so) or when you consider yourself to be in reasonably 'urgent' need of assistance. The message is the same as for the distress call, with the exception that the phrase Pan-Pan, repeated three times, is used instead of Mayday.

It's also a bright idea, when transmitting either of the above, to mention that you are a student pilot. The decks will then be cleared with some alacrity.

R/T COMMUNICATION

Some people find it easy to communicate with ATC; others don't. As we discussed earlier, what the brighter chaps do is pre-empt replies from the controller – rehearse in their minds the message they expect to receive – and thus not have to rattle off a great spiel from a single hearing. The gist of all communications is roughly the same from day to day – only barometric pressure, wind and runway in use alter. The bright ones, as I say, make themselves aware of all that before they go anywhere near the airfield. As you might have suspected, it always comes as a great new surprise to me.

Perhaps the easiest way to become familiar with r/t is buy an air-band radio. They're relatively cheap and they afford hours of homely fun. A number of manufacturers produce ABs specifically for enthusiasts, so you don't need to lash out on a massive set with all the gadgets and gizmos simply for the pleasure of listening to your student friends making unutterable twerps of themselves live.

When dealing with ATC, never be afraid to have a message repeated. And never be too proud to ask for assistance. After all, you can always hide behind that forgivable appellation 'student pilot'. It's the finest excuse for cock-ups since Napoleon got indigestion at the gates of Moscow. I have it on the very best authority that ATC are there only to help, and under no circumstances will they bear a grudge.

To prove it, listen to this.

A certain student pilot, after a particularly stupid mistake in the air – one which brought him into conflict with ATC – was summoned to the tower to be given a rocket by the head man. There was said student trembling in his cotton socks, and there was controller X giving him the benefit of his non-regulation vocabulary.

Meanwhile, several hundred yards away, at a flying club which I have the decency not to name, another student was preparing to taxi to the holding point. It was a journey that would take him past the tower.

Now, light aircraft, being light, are usually lashed down when not in use; i.e. two ropes attached to anchor-rings in the ground are tied to eyelets beneath each wing, and the plane is held fast. On some fields, the anchor rings are set into movable concrete blocks, thus to facilitate parking anywhere and everywhere.

Wait for it.

Back at the tower, student No. 1 is bravely accepting his lambasting and doing his best to hold back the tears, when beneath the tower window trundles student pilot No. 2, complete with a hundredweight concrete block trailing the ground from each wing! As you can imagine, it brought the house down. What could controller X do but curl up?

On another occasion, ATC were experiencing a problem communicating with a student in the air. He continually went on and off mike the way actors do to establish distance in radio drama, and he appeared to the people on the ground to be under some strain. When they eventually got his undivided attention, he admitted to having dropped his cigarette, which he couldn't reach, and the carpet was smouldering.

'Never mind,' said the controller coolly. 'You're OK. The carpets of your aircraft are fire-proofed.' To which he added: 'You may, however, experience some slight asphyxia.'

And then, while we're on the subject, there was the British Airways Shuttle skipper who had a comical turn of mind. It's common practice that controllers will ask incoming pilots, after landing, to declare their intentions, to which the pilot will announce that he's turning right at the first exit, carrying on to the end of the runway, back-tracking or whatever. Anyway, when they asked this particular Trident captain his intentions, he said: 'Well, I'm going to taxi to the terminal, unload the passengers and have a cup of tea. Then I think I'll jet me back to London.'

Incidentally, it's always a good idea to know that your radio is working properly. To find out, all you have to do is ask. The reply you get will be one of the following: 1. Unreadable. 2. Readable now and then. 3. Readable, but with difficulty. 4. Readable. 5. Perfectly readable.

Readability will be given as a strength using the appropriate figure as above.

PHONETIC ALPHABET

Here's where you brush up, or learn, your phonetic alphabet.

Letter	*Word*	*Letter*	*Word*
A	Alpha	N	November
B	Bravo	O	Oscar
C	Charlie	P	Papa
D	Delta	Q	Quebec
E	Echo	R	Romeo
F	Foxtrot	S	Sierra
G	Golf	T	Tango
H	Hotel	U	Uniform
I	India	V	Victor
J	Juliet	W	Whisky
K	Kilo	X	X-ray
L	Lima	Y	Yankee
M	Mike	Z	Zulu

THE COMEDY OF ERRORS

Every pilot is required to keep a log of his flying activities. These are recorded in a special logbook during flight or immediately after. Your instructor will keep yours up to date during training. He probably won't let you take charge of it until you've obtained your licence, on account of you'll only use it to impress your friends (students are like that) and almost certainly lose it somewhere embarrassing. Imagine the red face when it's returned from the local bawdy-house.

Back to the logbook. It should contain details of all your flights as a crew member: dates, times, durations, aircraft registration marks and the capacity in which you acted – e.g. commander. (Doesn't that sound good?) Besides the log-book, your instructor also keeps a detailed log of your performance while training. Each of the fifteen or so air exercises you undertake will be noted and commented upon by him. I urge you not to try to sneak a look at your performance log while his back is turned. It could mean the end of self-respect and confidence as you know it; his remarks on paper may be even more lurid than those he uses during exercises.

SPECIAL EQUIPMENT

Aside from the aviation books you buy to advance your own knowledge privately, you will need a few items of equipment for use during ground-school training and afterwards when you have your wings.

An Airtour slide-rule computer is a must, as are the relevant aviation charts of your flying region, a scale-ruler, a protractor, a knee-pad and some chinagraph pencils.

At today's prices, that little lot will set you back roughly the equivalent of an hour's dual flying time. Not a lot to pay for what you get; and what you get is a set of equipment (charts aside, since they need updating) to last a lifetime.

RUNWAYS

The following may seem rather obvious to most people, yet there are a few, myself included, who may never have given a previous thought to it. The subject in question is runway alignment.

Why does a given runway travel in one particular direction when at another airfield five miles away it heads off in a different direction? The answer, not unreasonably, is that runways are aligned to take advantage of the prevailing wind. Airfield planners have the happy knack of positioning runways in such a way that ninety-nine times out of a hundred an aircraft can take off and land directly, or as near as doesn't matter, into wind.

A similar thought worthy of mention is the numbering of runways. From what I know of you, you are by no means such a twit as not to realize that runways are aligned to compass bearings. (You bought this book, so you can't be.) Given this to be a fact, on both counts, it follows that runway 26 is plumbed in to the bearing 260°. Its reciprocal 08, conversely, is lined up on 080°. What an incredible number of people fail to grasp during the early stages of training is the elementary truth that the number indicates the direction in which the runway is travelling. Hence, the number announces the beginning of the runway and points its direction (see Fig. 23).

Palpably self-evident, isn't it?

What may not be so obvious about runways are the following observations:

1. A runway that has a slope of as little as 2° can extend the take-off run by ten per cent.
2. A grass runway can add as much as eighteen per cent to take-off distance.
3. The higher the elevation of a runway, the longer the take-off run. That's because the density of air decreases with altitude, so you need extra thrust for a standard amount of lift.
4. A runway situated in a cold climate offers a better take-off performance than one in a warm climate. The higher the temperature, the lower the air density.
5. Take-off run details given by aircraft manufacturers shouldn't be confused with take-off distance. Take-off run is shorter, because take-off distance is measured from initial roll to fifty feet above ground level.

A VISUAL AID AND MEMORY JOGGER

In the initial stages of flying training, it often happened that I would lose my bearings when approaching the home airfield. And now I come to think about it, it almost *always* happened.

The fact is, things tend to look different from the air. What's more, they seem to change, literally, with the weather. A touch of ground haze and landmarks melt into the background or, in extreme cases, disappear altogether – this includes the airfield itself. A vivid sun, and things which 'weren't there the last time' suddenly materialize.

What I found most difficult was working out the configuration of the runways if I approached from a direction previously not flown, or if ATC suddenly decided to switch me to a runway other than the one I'd taken off from. Indeed, and I'm loath to admit it, I even got mixed up when doing nothing more adventurous than simply taxi-ing the aircraft across to the other side of the field to pick up fuel.

Anyway, I resolved the problem by drawing up the runway

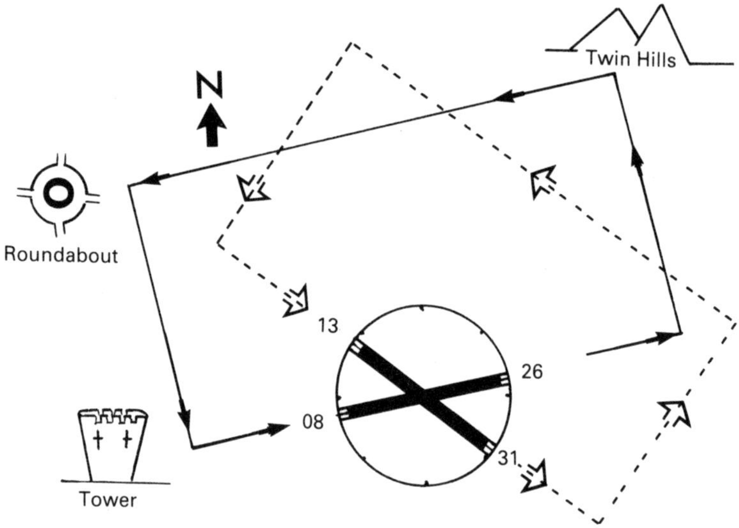

Fig. 21. Runway layout and circuit landmarks

layout on a piece of 3″ × 11″ card and orienting it to magnetic north. I then included landmarks within the circuit area, and added a note of the various radio frequencies, Air Traffic Zone reporting points, plus the gist of TMPFF and BUMPFF.

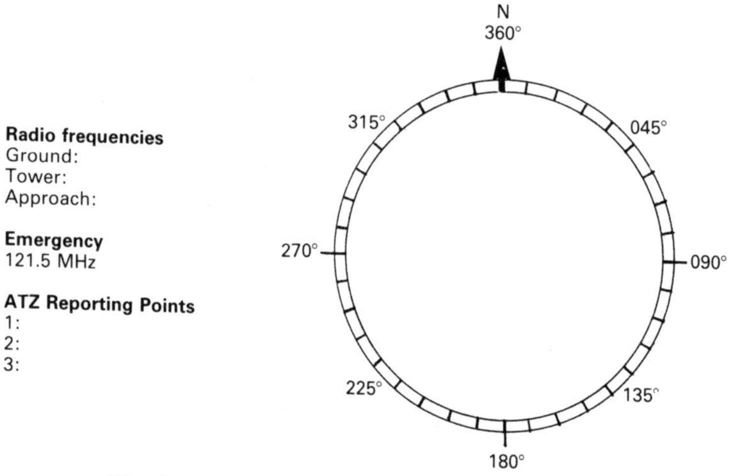

Fig. 22. Draw in your runways and landmarks

The card was then folded as a gatefold – i.e. six pages – which fitted neatly into a shirt pocket. This memory jogger went everywhere with me for the first couple of months, and it was invaluable.

You can make up your own visual aid by photocopying the 360° 'compass' below and drawing in your own runways and landmarks. Thus, all you have to do when approaching the field – when you're a mile or two distant – is orient north on the card with 360° on your DI . . . and all should become clear. You may also wish to add radio frequencies and so on.

NOW TAKE YOUR MOCK EXAM

So as to give you a taste of what's to come, here are some questions along the lines of those you'll be set in the various written exams. I should stress that the following are not taken from existing papers and should be viewed as examples only. Fortunately, most questions in all three papers are of the multiple choice variety – so the correct answer is there somewhere!

Airframes and Engines

1. In banking an aircraft to the right, the ailerons are positioned thus:
   (a) Port aileron up, starboard aileron down.
   (b) Starboard aileron up, port aileron down.
   (c) Both ailerons neutral.
2. Flaps are fitted to an aircraft so as to:
   (a) Increase stalling angle, lift and drag.
   (b) Increase stalling speed and lift, while moving centre of pressure rearward.
   (c) Increase lift and drag while lowering stalling speed.
3. The Air Speed Indicator of a flying machine is operated by:
   (a) Static vent.
   (b) Pitot tube.
   (c) Both the above.
4. Should the static vent become blocked in flight, thus rendering the altimeter unserviceable, what is the immediate course of action?

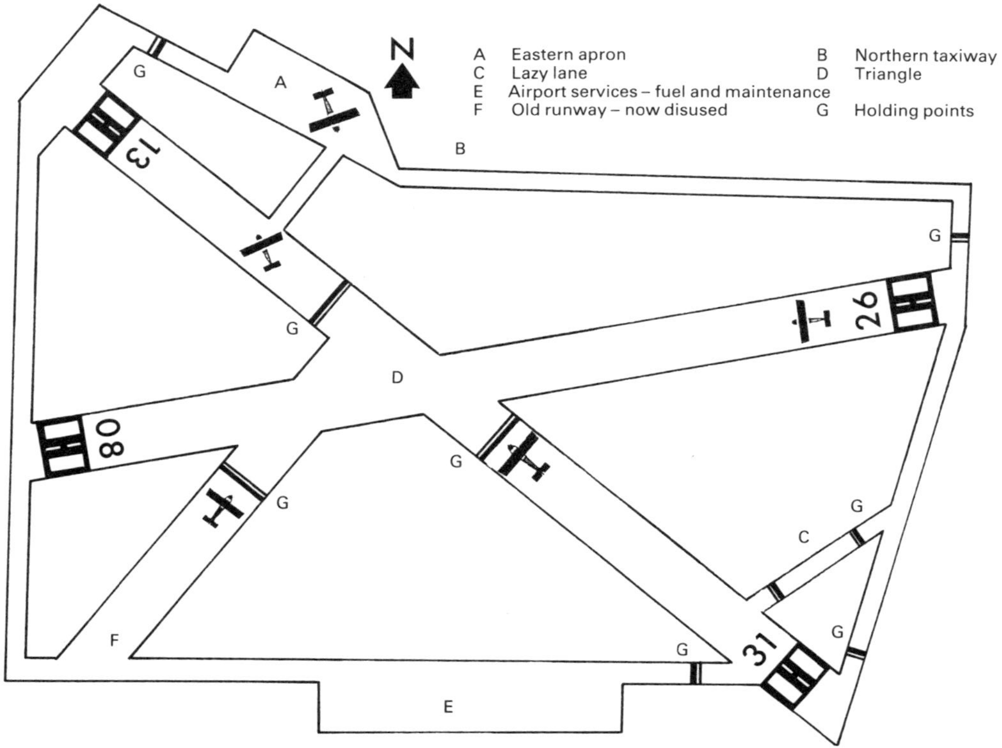

Fig. 23. Typical airfield layout. This happens to be a two-thirds representation of Edinburgh Airport. Runways 25/07 are missing

(a) Continue the flight and maintain safe height by visual reference to the ground.
(b) Land as soon as safely possible.
(c) Break the glass of a pressure instrument to restore correct outside pressure.

5. When approaching the stall, the flight characteristics are:
   (a) The angle of attack increases while the centre of pressure moves forward.
   (b) The angle of attack increases while the centre of pressure moves rearward.
   (c) The angle of attack decreases while the centre of gravity moves forward.

Answers. Question: 1. (b). 2. (c). 3. (c). 4. (c) The glass to break is that of the Vertical Speed Indicator, since it's the least important of the pressure instruments. 5. (a).

Navigation and Meteorology

1. When air density is reduced below International Standard Atmosphere, what effect will it have on take-off run?
   (a) Shorter take-off run.
   (b) Longer take-off run.
   (c) No difference.
2. Given a True Heading of 108°, a Variation of 10° West and a Deviation of 2° East, what is the Compass heading?
   (a) 116°
   (b) 117°
   (c) 120°
3. Winds in an anticyclone or high-pressure area circulate in a clockwise direction and are said to be:
   (a) Backing.
   (b) Veering.
   (c) Falling.
4. A pilot would be more likely to expect severe turbulence, icing and thunderstorms in which type of cloud?
   (a) Cirrocumulus.
   (b) Altocumulus.
   (c) Cumulonimbus.
5. On a given day, an airfield has a QFE of 995 millibars and a QNH of 1000 millibars. What is the airfield's height above sea-level?

(a) 150 feet.
(b) 50 feet
(c) 15 feet.

6. After flying for fifteen miles on a sixty-mile leg, a pilot finds himself three miles to port of his Required Track. Using the 1-in-60 rule, calculate the track error:
   (a) 6°
   (b) 4°
   (c) 12°

Answers. Question: 1. (b). 2. (a). 3 (b). 4. (c). 5. (a). 6. (c).

Aviation Law

1. The green starboard navigation light of an aircraft must be visible through:
   (a) 140°
   (b) 180°
   (c) 110°
2. A pilot may fly under Visual Flight Rules in controlled airspace provided he can remain:
   (a) One nautical mile horizontally and 1,000 feet vertically away from cloud and in a flight visibility of five nautical miles.
   (b) One nautical mile horizontally and 1,000 feet vertically away from cloud in a flight visibility of three nautical miles.
   (c) 1,000 feet vertically and 1,000 feet horizontally away from cloud in a flight visibility of one nautical mile.
3. When two aircraft are approaching head on, both shall alter course:
   (a) To port.
   (b) To starboard.
   (c) As deemed necessary.
4. An aircraft shall not fly closer to any person, vehicle or structure than:
   (a) 500 feet.
   (b) 1,000 feet.
   (c) 1,500 feet.
5. The visual or pyrotechnic signal indicating that an aircraft in the air should divert to another landing field is:
   (a) Continuous red luminous beam.

(b) Green pyrotechnic light or green flare.
(c) Intermittent red luminous beam.

Answers. Question: 1. (c). 2. (a). 3. (b). 4. (a). 5. (c).

(NOTE: The navigation and meteorology exams are separate papers. For brevity's sake, however, I have lumped them together here.)

Epilogue

If you've read this far without skipping bits, you ought by now to have a working knowledge of PPL requirements. In any event, you should at least know more than when you started. If you don't, then I've put down fifty-odd thousand words for no good reason and you've blued the cover price. So go right on back and glean something – at least it will constitute a respectable grounding for when you join your flying club.

The purpose of this part of the book is to put the finishing touches to the work on your chimerical PPL; to run briefly through the final handling test; to discover how to apply for the licence; and to determine where we, or rather you, go from here.

THE TEST

The test lasts for anything up to an hour. An approved CAA examiner will conduct it if your instructor isn't qualified to do so. If he is, you're on the pig's back; but if you do happen to draw a total stranger, don't on any account panic. He is well used to nervous students and he wants you to pass just as much as you do. Further, he is in the flying business rather than the failing business.

The exam programme starts from the minute you check into the flight room and either call or visit the local Met Office for a weather report. With good weather predicted, you will then be briefed by the examiner on what he wants you to do, where and how he wants you to do it, and the standard of flying he expects from you.

Out on the apron, he'll keep a hawklike eye on you as you conduct a full visual check of the aircraft. There's a precise drill for the job, whose dot-and-comma nature will already have been drummed into you via verbal and written checklists. Next you will be assessed on your start-up, r/t communication, taxi and vital actions procedures. You'll go through them strictly by the book; you will not deviate one whit from the holy writ. And that applies also to take-off, climb-out and exit from the zone.

Once in open country, you'll be asked to perform a series of manœuvres and they'll be exactly those you've been perfecting for months – stalls, tight turns, spins, emergency landing simulation, course-keeping and flying at minimum level.

All this while, you will be working like the clappers. Nerves will be violin-string taut, the fear of failure making your skin leak buckets. Strictly speaking, the chances of being back-squadded are not that great – unless of course you do something completely out of character, like passing out or climbing gibbering into the back of the plane and saying you don't want to play any more. After all, your instructor has his reputation to think of. He would be all kinds of a wally to refer you for a test you had no chance of passing.

At some time during the proceedings, you will surely be asked to undertake either a flapless landing or a performance landing. The first is obvious, the second isn't, because I've deliberately refrained from mentioning 'short-field' put-downs until now. The reason: they take longer to explain on paper than they take to achieve in practice. My sloth has now been found out and followed, so I'll explain.

A performance landing is one where you arrive on the concrete at the lowest possible speed and within the shortest possible distance. Otherwise known as a precautionary landing, it's basically as normal but with the flaps down as far as they will go – hanging off like decorations on a Christmas tree. The idea being that knowing how to land in limited space is insurance against the day you get an engine failure and have to do it for real, in someone's back yard.

Anyhow, let's assume you've galloped through the foregoing with no upset and you're feeling pretty happy with yourself – what comes next? Nothing more, in fact, than a first-class rejoin to the circuit, a better-than-average run-through of pre-landing vital actions, and a superb landing. This should be a doddle. You've been rehearsing it, dreaming it, eating, sleeping and drinking it for weeks. So you land, taxi back to the apron, perform a nonchalant shutdown, climb out and, with the suspense almost too much to bear, await delivery of the examiner's verdict.

If fortune is kind, and if the examiner feels he can allow you to become a licence-holder without his having to keep his fingers permanently crossed, you will be told there and then that you have succeeded.

All that remains is the licence application proper.

THE LICENCE

Given that you have £100 (that's the one-off fee at the time of writing) to chuck around, your instructor will send it, along with the related documents (logbook, exam papers, progress sheets, etc) to the CAA licensing authority. If everything is above board, you'll receive a plastic folder – not unlike a driving-licence holder – containing your PPL.

And thereby hangs the anticlimax. For the money, you will very likely be expecting a leather-bound, hand-tooled, gold-embossed passport of the air, or similar. No such luck, I'm afraid. It seems to me that all the character has gone out of bureaucracy these days and you rarely get what you pay for in documentary terms.

Still, initial disappointment aside, what do you really care. You have your licence, and you'd accept it on newsprint if that's how it came. And I for one wouldn't blame you.

WHAT NEXT?

So *quo vadis*? A good and timely question. You have your PPL; you are at liberty to do anything aeronautical within the meaning of the act; you are cock-a-hoop and grandiloquent to a fault. Where do you go from here?

To start with, I suppose, you'll want to take the family up into the air – if only to prove that all those evenings when you said you were attending ground-school classes weren't in reality spent boozing with the boys, or the girls. Next, you will doubtless wish to spread your wings and explore farther afield. Trips to the Isle of Man, for instance, or the Isle of Capri, providing you can find it on the map.

Flying clubs, if they are any good, periodically organize rallies and fly-ins. The former are events featuring competition-flying between clubs, and the latter a case of paying flying visits to clubs at other fields where, with any luck, you will be treated right royally for the evening or weekend.

For this type of activity, you will hire aircraft by the hour from your club. And note that you are expected to pay only for flying time – time in the air. Any time spent on the ground is for free.

Most PPLs are happy with the club-hire situation. A few, a happy few, manage to acquire their own aircraft. Situated somewhere between these two groups is a fraternity which gets the best of both worlds by group-sharing aircraft. The idea is that half-a-dozen or so flyers get together and buy an aircraft outright. From then on, they share running costs and maintenance costs and work to a roster for flying time. Schemes along these lines operate very smoothly – just so long as everybody plays the game.

One other side of the PPL coin is the pilot who uses his licence for business travel. In this respect, the businessman and woman are not tied to scheduled airlines.

But will you, I ask, be content to bash around in your single-engine job until you yourself sprout wings? Not Pygmalion likely, you won't. Because the throb of twin engines will be siren music to your ears and you'll be casting around for some likely idiot who owns a Cougar or a Cessna 340 to let you have a go.

To pick up a Twin Rating means half-a-dozen hours of dedicated graft. It also means the thick end of £1,000 to get those hours in. But if you're very, very lucky and your instructor thinks you're worth the bother, you may just be able to fly a few of those hours buckshee. Here's how.

All aircraft of whatever type have to undergo periodic checks – services, if you like. Now the chances of a club having the proper servicing facility right there on the field are fairly remote. So planes have to be delivered to and collected from other establishments for the work to be carried out. Clearly some lucky devil has to do the delivering and collecting. As I say, if your instructor is a half-decent bloke who wants you to get on, you'll maybe have the opportunity to accompany him and thus log the time.

I'll say here and now that flying twins is a knock-out. Engines have to be operated in strict co-ordination, undercarriages have to be lowered, you deal with things like rudder trim as well as elevator trim, and there's that much more to it to challenge the keen pilot. Believe me, the first time you drop the wheels and see three green lights on the dashboard is sheer poetry. You feel like a pilot in every sense of the word.

On the other hand, of course, your ambitions may be confined to singles where you fancy obtaining a Night Rating or an Instrument Meteorological Conditions Rating – both of which are well worth having and can do you nothing but good from an airmanship point of view. For all I know, you may be even more enterprising and want to go for a Commercial Pilot's Licence. Good for you.

As a matter of fact, no matter how old or young you are, the sky is far from being the limit to your aspirations. There is so much more to do and so much more to conquer. Having got this far, you'll want to go on and on . . . and on, especially if you find a good club and a compatible instructor. As I said right at the beginning, the bloke who sets out to teach you to fly can make you or break you. So his response and interest depend on your attitude. I have heard people, who really ought to know better, telling their instructor that they are employing him and by that token suggesting he is there for no other reason than to provide a service. These types don't usually get very far, invariably leaving the club and moaning about its standards to anyone who'll listen.

So take my tip. Treat the man as though he knows more than you'll ever know. You'll be not only absolutely and categorically right but also a very good pupil.

I leave you with this thought. Flying will be the most interesting business you've ever undertaken – that's a promise. But now you must promise me something: that you will avoid the following basic pilot errors – 1. Overconfidence. 2. Haste. 3. Distraction. 4. Unfamiliarity.

If you have been, thanks for reading. And if you care to, please let me know how you get on.

Abbreviations

AIAA	Area of Intense Aerial Activity
AMSL	Above Mean Sea Level
ASI	Airspeed Indicator
ATC	Air Traffic Control
APT	Attitude. Power. Trim
ATZ	Aerodrome Traffic Zone
BUMPFF	Brakes off. Undercarriage down. Mixture rich. Pitch. Flaps. Fuel
CAA	Civil Aviation Authority
CASH	Cirrus. Alto. Stratus. Heaped (Cumulus)
CDMVT	Compass. Deviation. Magnetic. Variation. True
DI	Direction Indicator
HASELL	Height. Airframe. Security. Engine. Location. Look out
IAS	Indicated airspeed
IMC	Instrument Meteorological Conditions
MATZ	Military Air Traffic Zone
NFT	Navigation Flight Test.
PAT	Power. Attitude. Trim
PPL	Private Pilot's Licence
QFE	Atmospheric pressure at airfield elevation
QNH	Atmospheric pressure at sea level
RT	Radio Telephone
SPL	Student Pilot's Licence
TAS	True Airspeed
TMPFF	Trim. Mixture. Pitch. Fuel. Flaps
UTC	Universal Co-ordinated Time
VFR	Visual Flight Rules
VMC	Visual Meteorological Conditions
VSI	Vertical Speed Indicator

Bibliography

The following is a short list of books that should help make the student pilot's life that much easier. Some are highly technical; some are simply light reading with an aviation bias; and one or two are a sheer delight.

Murchie, Guy, *The World Aloft* (Bantam Books)

W. H. Birch and A. E. Bramson, *Flight Briefing for Pilots*, eight volumes (Pitman)

M. Gibson and M. Harrison, *Into Thin Air: The History of Aviation Medicine* (Robert Hale)

A. E. Bramson, *Make Better Landings* (Martin Dunitz)

Ronald Hurst and Leslie Hurst, *Pilot Error* (Granada)

Civil Aviation Authority, *The Private Pilot's Licence & Associated Ratings*

Civil Aviation Authority, *Radiotelephony*.

Pilot (monthly), 88 Burlington Road, New Malden, Surrey, KT3 4NT

Jerram, Mike, *To Be a Pilot* (Airlife Publications)

Campbell, Ron, *Flying and Ground Training* (6 volumes, Granada).

Thom, Trevor, *Air Pilot's Manuals* (5 volumes, Airlife Publications)

Cassette Tapes

Airtape (Publications) Ltd: Complete PPL package (6 cassettes), ATPL, Denham Aerodrome, Uxbridge, Middlesex UB9 5DE

Airtour Audio Training Tapes, all subjects. Elstree Aerodrome, Hertfordshire

Index

Q. Assuming standard atmospheric conditions calculate the TAS of aircraft ~~traveling~~ flying at 30,000ft at Mach 0.9. Assume speed of sound may be calculated from formula

$$662 \times \sqrt{\frac{\text{Temp}^\circ\text{c} + 273}{288}} \text{ knots}$$

A. ISA at Sea level temp = +15°c

Reduction = 1.98° per ~~[illegible]~~ 1000ft.

Temp at 30 000ft = 15°c − (1.98 × 30)

= 15 − 59.4

= −44°

Speed of sound = $662\sqrt{\frac{-44+273}{288}}$ = 590 knots

(590 × 1.15 = 678.5 mph.)

TAS = Speed of Sound × Mach No

= 590 × 0.9 = 531 knots approx 600 mph.

- Mach number = $\frac{\text{TAS}}{\text{Speed of Sound}}$
- Speed of sound at Sea level 15° = 662 kts